I DON'T BELONG HERE

I DON'T BELONG HERE

CARL SHEFFIELD

Charleston, SC
www.PalmettoPublishing.com

I Don't Belong Here
Copyright © 2023 by Carl Sheffield

First Edition

Hardcover ISBN: 979-8-8229-1874-0
Paperback ISBN: 979-8-8229-1875-7
eBook ISBN: 979-8-8229-1876-4

CONTENTS

SYNOPSIS

By request of my mother and father, I was asked to explore the regions of space. My destination was the Milky Way galaxy. My journey would lead me to several places of the outer reaches of space. My quest would carry me to planets one could only dream of—and some not so friendly. This was a journey I would finish for my mother and father, the queen and king of Ticoru. There was no way to know what would happen; there was no way to see what lie ahead. On this quest, I would learn the cold, hard facts of life—I would experience death, the destruction of my ship, and the loss of my friends. On earth I would discover that I do not belong here as I did on other worlds, but I would find a dear friend on this planet called earth—I would find the love of my life and the future queen of Ticoru.

CHAPTER 1

OPENING MY EYES, I FOUND MYSELF LYING ON THE floor. Placing my arms on my bed, I pulled myself to a sitting position. My vision was blurry; many thoughts flashed through my mind. The only thing I could think was: what happened? I tried to stand; my body trembled. Slowly the surroundings were coming to me. I thought of the crew. Opening the door and gazing down the corridor, I ran from one wall to the other until I reached the bridge.

The corridor was filled with the lingering smell of smoke. How long had I been out? Several members of the crew were dead or dying. Shaking my head to clear my thoughts, I realized we had been attacked again. It was not the first time—I was not sure who this was or why they kept attacking us; I suppose they felt as if we were a threat. My pilot kept eluding them, yet they follow.

My crew had fought hard. The ones that died from the explosion and the ones that were dying will always be remembered. I will place this in my captain's log; each one died with honor, each hand-picked by my father.

I tried to help all I could to ease the pain of my crew. The ship was my first concern; space alone is sudden death without a ship in working condition.

I called out to what remained of the crew and asked for a damage report. It was said by one that we had taken some damage to the hull of the ship; that section was closed off. For the time we were alive and safe.

I took a walk through the ship trying to help with the removal of the debris; I surely did not want to find another crew member under the wreckage. Making a full inventory of the crew and the ship, I walked down the corridor with thoughts in my head—nine crew members gone, and for what? Looking through a window portal, I could see the parcel damage of the ship. I was the captain; I should have more knowledge of the ship.

Several hours had passed since the attack. My pilot took control of the ship as I excused myself. I made my way to my quarters, trying to understand the events of the day as it is in space, since it is always dark. My thoughts went to my home, my mother, and my father—I suppose they would be happy of the way I was changing; the man I am becoming.

Sitting at my desk looking out the portal window, I noticed the stars had a different glow. They seemed to have a more brilliant glow. We were still in the same universe, yet something was different. During the attack without noticing, did we cross a cosmic line? I was not sure of this, yet here we are.

I decided to go to the galley for tea. Walking down the corridor, a trace of charred smoke lingered as I passed several pieces of debris that had not been removed; I heard someone call me. Turning, I saw no one. I was pouring my tea when the bridge called, and I left in a hurry to the bridge. Entering the bridge, the crew was working to clean the floors and walls from the attack. The pilot told me he had full control of the ship. "The ship's hull had a rip, captain; it looks as if a laser hit us."

I ask, "Did anyone see a ship?" The crew looked at me without answering. I knew a ship was there, but who was it and why were they attacking us?

I walked to the table where the star charts were. Taking a scroll, I rolled it out. I had no clue where we were going. In space, you relied on your star charts and sometimes your imagination. I learned this in my training; I never realized I would ever need it—I was a prince and the son of a king and queen. I was thankful for the training. Our mission was to seek out a planet in the Milky Way galaxy. In my thoughts, I wondered if such a place even existed. I had been only to one other planet since my birth. I stood beside my father when I was six as he was welcome by the governor of the planet of Makar. Returning home, I never left Ticoru until

I embarked on this mission by my father's request; he said it would be good for me. Since I had no mate, I accepted the mission—two years we have been gone. We have been attacked by this ship several times and in my thoughts, I would never see Ticoru again.

My thoughts seemed to escape me again; I was sitting on the fertile hillside overlooking the valley of Ticoru, a place I often went to when I wished to be alone. Ticoru was a beautiful world—we were a free world; it was a place where we could come and go as we please.

Taking my tea in hand and having a sip, my thoughts suddenly went to the voice in the corridor. Who called me? I saw no one there. Setting my tea on the table, I turned as the navigator called: "Captain, we have a ship showing on the scope. Captain, it appears to be the same ship."

Who are these beings? Why are they following us? Why were they attacking us? I turned to look at the scope again; they were coming fast. I called to the pilot: "Shields to full power."

"Sir, we do not have full power. Shields are at twenty percent. Captain, what is your order?" I told the pilot to stop the ship. "Sir," he replied.

The alien ship came around in a half-circle, sitting directly in front of us. I suppose this was it—I knew at this moment the blast would destroy us. I suppose here in the cold dark emptiness of space, this would be my destiny. Looking at the massive ship before us, a final round was coming. I knew in this moment I would never see Ticoru again. Believe me—I felt the pain in my heart for my crew.

Fighting a war on the ground was one thing; fighting in space was another. Here in the darkness of space there was no escape—if a ship explodes, there was no escaping death. If the explosion did not kill you, the cold, dark space would kill you in seconds. Floating in space, you would freeze as solid as the ice lakes high in the mountains of Ticoru.

Ticoru had a tropical valley. The mountains were so high. The frozen lakes supplied the water to the fertile valleys that made Ticoru a tropical paradise. My father would tell me of other worlds he visited on some of his journeys. He would say, "My son, some worlds are very primitive. Some worlds are so advanced and some have no technology at all—they are simple people." He would say there were other species on these worlds but this did not have a bearing on me. Ticoru had several species; I do remember my father told me in a council meeting we were called humans. I had no way to verify this, since I had lived there my whole life. Humans have come to our world from time to time, yet, so did other species.

Twenty-two years ago, I was born to my parents. I was given the name of Paxton. It was not a common name, but it was my name—I was proud of this name they gave me. Father said it was a strong name.

The king of our world was called Oron. His queen, Amore, was always by his side. I was proud to say they were my mother and father. Being a prince never meant much to me; I wanted to be me.

In the chambers of our council, where this mission was discussed, my father stood. "I have a captain in arms for this mission; I will send my son Paxton. He is capable and has study of star charts—this will be good for him." Why we wanted to go to this Milky Way galaxy was beyond me. Father said we need to explore; I did not see the irony in it. On Ticoru we had all we needed—what could we possible need from this Milky Way galaxy? Looking back on all that had happened, I wish to be back on Ticoru.

This was a strange journey I was on. How could I lead my crew after this? I feel I have let everyone down, staring at the scope waiting for the end; thoughts escaped me once more. I went to the voice in the corridor. Who called to me— it was a female voice? I could not understand the voice. I thought, could this be my mother trying to reach me? The voice called so softly as a whisper on the valley winds of my world. "Paxton—be strong; stand tall." My mother was strong in mind thoughts, like she could see the future. I could do this too, sometimes—this was not one of those times, or at least I thought. I closed my eyes, opening them as the alien ship pulled away. Why could I not say? I watched it as it went to hyperspace. My crew turned to me, as if I made the ship leave.

My pilot ask, "Captain, what happened?"

I replied, "I cannot say. Let us get underway. We will not see them again for some time." Looking at me, heads were shaking, shoulders shrugging as we were underway. I told everyone, "Let us try to repair what we can. Hopefully, we will find a friendly planet soon."

Following the encounter of the alien ship, two days passed as it was in space. I was resting when I was called to the bridge. The pilot told me there was a planet two days away. Traveling at the speed we were traveling, that was still a long way off.

My thought went to the alien ship. Why did it leave? Where did it go? I feel maybe it is somewhere in space, waiting. There was nothing on the scope—we were not being followed; we were alone here in the darkness of space, a place that seemed to have no end—an endless place where you were always alone.

Since our first attack, I wondered who these beings were. I know it was no enemy of mine or my father. Sitting here, I found it hard to imagine the pain of my crew; the lives lost. Some of them had lived together all their lives—they were dear friends and family. Would I ever live to return to Ticoru? Being the captain, I should make a turn and go home; home to my world; home to Ticoru.

I told my pilot as I left the bridge that I would retire to my quarters. I made tea and studied the star charts. Looking out the portal window, somewhere in my thoughts, I fell asleep.

CHAPTER 2

MY EYES OPEN AS THE SHIP CAME FROM HYPER-space. Raising from the bed, I knew something had happened. What now?, I thought. I left my quarters to the corridor, walking fast to the bridge.

Entering the bridge I asked, "What now?"

Mora said, "Captain, we are surrounded by ships."

"Have they called us?" I ask.

"Nothing sir, they are just sitting there. It is like they are waiting to destroy us if we move."

I said, "Well, I suppose we need to sit still."

The pilot looked at me then said, "You think, sir?" Damn, I thought, we are dead. I told him, "We will wait."

The pilot asked, "Wait? Wait for what, sir?" The call came as I said that.

"UFO, you are in the moon's air space." I told the pilot: "This is what we are waiting on. Answer back." The pilot told me it should be me. "You are the captain."

"Who are you?" I asked. Replying, the speaker said, "We are from the Moon of Spores. You are surrounded." I told him, "We mean you no harm. We have been attacked by an unknow ship. We have damage to the ship and could use some help."

The voice asked, "Why are you here?" I told him we were on our way to the Milky Way galaxy. There was silence for several minutes. "Follow us to the surface," was the reply.

Time comes and goes; it has been over a year since we have been on ground of any kind. It would be good to stand on the ground; smell fresh air. The pilot followed the ship to the surface. We were instructed to land on a pad near a huge building and to land as close to the tracks as possible. The Spore's ship asked, "Captain, my governor would ask your name; he asked who attacked you?"

"I am called Paxton. My home world is Ticoru, far into the Kimura universe." I suppose this was sent to the floor of this moon. Once again, I was told to land as close to the tracks as possible. Coming through the atmosphere at sixty-five thousand feet, I only saw a speck of what I thought was a planet. The pilot slowed the ship as we were descending to the instruction pad.

Closer and closer we came as the pilot turned to land—I must say he did an excellent job; I could see why my father handpicked my crew. I could see several begin standing and waiting; it was as if they did not receive many ships, yet I found this hard to believe. There were too many pads here and they did have several ships. Well, I knew there were six.

There was one being that appeared to be as human as could be—well, he did appear that way to me. He was incredibly old; standing with a smile on his face as the ramp came down, there were others being there, too. I could say I had no clue who or what they were. I was told later they were called natives of the planet that disappeared.

Walking down the ramp, this old human greeted me. His hand extended with a smile. I could tell this human was a man of knowledge—there was no defying him. Looking into the eyes of this human I would not want to be on his bad side.

Taking my hand, he said, "I am called Cavota."

I took a quick look around at the beautiful place I stood; flashes went through my mind. I took the man's hand with a smile.

I answered back: "My name is Paxton; my home world is Ticoru." I kept talking, telling him we—my crew and I— are on our way to the Milky Way galaxy. I told him I was not sure why; this journey comes at my father request.

"My ship has been attacked several times by an unknown ship. I tell you now, I have no clue who this ship is or where it is from. One week ago, the last attack left us with severe damage to our hull; with regret I lost several crew members. They were good people."

I DON'T BELONG HERE

Cavota started the conversation. He said he knew about wars; he said the moon lived under Palatonians' laws for over three hundred years.

I asks, "You do not live under these laws now?"

Cavota told me of the planet that disappeared. He said they disappeared one night and no one knew where they went. King Zin, the ruler, said he did not wish to have war with anyone then later one night, he made the planet disappear. The system they went to became too hot, so he moved the planet back here to the Spores galaxy. Upon moving back, King Zin destroyed Plano—this is where the Palatonians were from. Of course, he destroyed several other planets; he took a band of warriors through a portal to do just that.

I looked at this human—and now, I was not so sure he was old. I looked at him with a skeptical look. "A portal, you say? I have no idea what you are saying. Is this thing you call a portal—is it real?"

Cavota said, "I can assure you portals are real. King Zin creates them with the power he has. Of course, with the staff of Ira." I had to ask, "Where is this planet now and what is this Staff of Ira?"

Cavota told me Zin had relocated the planet again, this time moving to the Claxton galaxy—this was the third time he had moved the planet.

I said, "When he wants, he just moves a planet?" Well in my mind, I thought, how can you move a planet?

Cavota smiled, "Paxton, my newfound friend, you do not know the power these people have. Zin has the power. He moved so they did not have to fight with the outside world. He comes here and is always watching us through his portal. We are not the only ones; there are several planets he watches." Cavota and I talked for several hours; he told me to have my people come ashore. Cavota give us refuge in a large building that we found accommodating.

Cavota said this was a moon, but I was not sure of this— if it were, it was like no moon I knew of. Here it was so green and marvelous. Cavota told me the story of his grandfather that started the moon from nothing—of course, it was with the help of the natives of the planet that disappeared, known as Boldlygo. Several hundred years passed then to my father, Alex, then to me.

The mornings come and goes like the wind blowing. Where does it go? We had been here on the moon with Cavota for over a week. I really wanted my ship repaired; I wanted to be on my way to this Milky Way galaxy.

Cavota told me in one of our counsels that we were on the right track to the Milky Way galaxy. It lies in the galaxy of a planet we used to travel to, called Earth. He told me Earth was a beautiful planet, yet humans are primitive.

I asked, "Have you been to this planet called Earth?" Cavota told me he has never left the moon except once, and that was to go to Boldlygo. King Zin brought several planets' leaders there to form an alliance; he brought some of them through his portal. There were others who came by ship.

Cavota was showing me around when a sentry appeared and whispered in his ear something I could not understand.

Cavota glanced at me with a look. "My friend, it appears we have visitors in space. My ships have surrounded a ship. There has been no communication except…" "Except what?" I asked.

Cavota replied, "They asked about you—they did not ask about you by name, just of the ship. They asked why we help you."

I said, "Cavota, I tell you, sir, I do not know these beings—whoever they are."

Cavota said, "I do believe you, Paxton." Cavota stood and so did I. Cavota and I walked to the door of the prison we were touring. He told the sentry to tell them to land and if they fire, we will destroy them. The sentry replied as he left: "As you wish, sir."

As Cavota instructed, the message was delivered to the ship. Cavota told me we should return to the council chambers—whoever this is will be escorted to the chambers. He said, "I assure you the ship will land." I give him a doubting look. "Really," I said.

"My new-found friend, I will have a council with these beings. I assure you if they do not land, they will be destroyed' my pilots are exceptionally good at what they do. I promise you I will find out why they attack your ship."

Cavota called to his captain, "Bring the ship into port; no shuttle. Have their pilot land on the north pad." Gazing skyward at a loud sound like an explosion, a ship came through the atmosphere. I watched as the ship made its descent to the pad—it looks bigger in live view. Finally sitting down on the pad, Cavota started toward the ship then stopped. "You coming?" he asked.

Walking to the ship, my thought was that I wanted to know why they kept attacking me; I also wanted to know who they were. Looking around at this place—a moon, as Cavota said it was—I only knew one thing: I do not belong here.

CHAPTER 3

A GENTLE BREEZE BLEW FROM THE EDGE OF THE landing pads; it was the first time I felt this sensation on this world. We continued to the pad. The breeze reminded me of home; the breeze that blew from the mountains. I would sit on the veranda overlooking the mountains. I also had a beautiful view of the city that seemed to come alive with life—ships would come and go, bringing imports from other planets, other worlds, then the ships would return to the cold, dark emptiness of space. I suppose I was in a daze; Cavota called me twice before I acknowledged him.

Cavota said, "You were lost in thought, Paxton. It is not good to go deep like that." I told him I went home; that I do not belong here. Cavota placed his hand on my shoulder. "Shall we see what they want?"

The big ship sat for several minutes. The hatch from the big ship came down as several of the crew walked down the ramp. Behind the crew walked a being that was not human— nor was the crew after further inspection. What appeared to be the leader was inches taller than the others and he walked with authority. He was broad at the shoulders; a long cape dragged the ramp as he walked to Cavota. Looking upon him, I did not know this being, nor had I ever met him. I cannot remember them ever coming to our world.

Nearing the end of the ramp, he began to speak: "I am called Kalean." I was surprised to hear he could speak our words. Cavota replied by saying who he was; Kalean told Cavota he was not accustomed to being told what to do.

Cavota smiled, "Sir, there is a first time for everything. You, sir, may come ashore with one crew member." Cavota give a sentry an order; several sentries circled around the ship.

Kalean asks, "Why the hostility?"

Cavota said, "One never knows. You have tried to destroy this man's ship on several occasions."

Kalean replied, "There is no disrespect here; we destroy all that define us."

Cavota said, "Yes, so did the Centaurians and Palatonians. They were destroyed."

Well, I took that to be an invitation. "Who are you?" I asked. "I do not know you; I have surely never seen you and I certainly do not wish for a war. My crew and I are on a mission to the Milky Way galaxy—we wish no harm to anyone, yet you have killed several of my crew with these attacks."

I was about to say something else when the entire world lit up in a bluish gray light. To me this was frightening, especially when heavily-armed sentries stepped through, followed by a man and a woman. You could tell this was a king and queen. This hole in the middle of the pad closed. Several people, including Cavota, kneeled. Since I had no clue what was going on, I did the same.

I looked upward as the person spoke to Cavota. "Rise Cavota, there is no reason for you to kneel before me."

Cavota answered, "As you wish, King Zin." Well, I will say, I was impressed. Cavota had spoken of Zin on several occasions. Finally, I will meet this wonder of the Planet of Boldlygo. I turned to see where Kalean was; he was standing with a gaze on his face. I do believe he was somewhat in shock.

Cavota introduced me to Zin. Cavota told Zin of the troubles I had with Kalean's ship. Zin told us the ship had been reported by the satellite in space.

The woman who was introduced as Zin's queen stood close to his side. I had seen, in the past, my mother do the same to my father.

Zin turned to look at Kalean. "Sir, I do believe we should have a council."

Cavota said, "The chambers has been prepared."

Smiling, Zin said, "So Cavota, you knew I would come."

Kalean said, "I will wait here. I need no counselling."

Zin replied, "the council is for you and what we should do of your behavior. You see, you are in a galaxy where I protect my people from being like you. We—here on the moon, as several other planets—have an alliance; we do not tolerate war. I promise you I will take everything you think you have—even your life if necessary. Shall we go?" Well, you could tell from the expression this did not sit well with Kalean.

Kalean said something in a language I did not understand then stepped from the ramp. We made our way to the chambers where the council was held. Since my stay here, I had only been in this room once. I was impressed by the graphics of the room. I thought, Who thinks of things like this? It was very impressive.

Cavota spoke for several minutes then asked Zin to speak. Zin let go of the arm of his queen. He introduced the ones that came from the hole in the air he called a portal—this was still hard for me to understand. He introduced Tressa first. Tressa's eyes were as blue as the sky of Ticoru. There was also Basco, Adair, Dorn, Leah, and Kar. From looking at these people, I would not want to be on their bad side.

Each person smiled, bowed, and said hello. Kalean was looking doubtful, like "I am in charge here." Kalean spoke out with a stern voice: "Stupid formalities. Your race is so weak. This makes me the superior."

Zin said, "I know who you are. Once, when I was a small child, I came to your planet." The woman Leah, whom Zin introduced, gave Zin a skeptical look. I did not know at the time she was his mother. Zin told Kalean that his race was strong; you could tell this pleased Kalean. Zin asked, "Kalean, can your race create portals? Can you or your race destroy a planet with a signal blow? If not, that makes me the superior one."

"I am the king of my world. The person to my left is King Kar; he is the king of the Claxtons of Galaxo in the Claxton galaxy. Together, we are more powerful than you could possibly imagine."

I am not sure how things happen; I only know they do. Zin started to speak when the sound of a ship roared. The sound shook the ground and the building of council. I tell you I have heard several ships ignite in my life—this one was furious. Kalean's ship was trying to leave. From nowhere, seven ships appeared—that ship wasn't getting far.

I left in a run with a sentry in lead and Cavota beside me. Through the doorway as fast as I could run, I saw the moon ships hoovering over Kalean's ship. Looking up I knew the only place the ship was going was down. Cavota instructed his captain, "Have them land or be destroyed."

The ship touched down and sentries surrounded the ship as others removed the crew to a large building. Zin and I walked onto the ship followed by Cavota. Looking to the bridge, I thought, nice, indeed. Zin read my thoughts. "I agree," he said.

CHAPTER 4

INSIDE THE CHAMBERS, I TOOK THE TIME BEFORE the council continued to talk to the others. I found it very inspiring. Cavota told Kalean it was very stupid to do what he had instructed his captain to do.

Kalean said, "I was checking."

Cavota asks, "What were you checking, to see what kind of security I have? Well, Kalean, I am sure you find it to be most impressive."

Zin started to speak again. "As I started to say, Kalean, before we were interrupted—I as a small child—with the help of Mya, Bota, and Maoke—were searching for a universe to move our people; a place where we could live without war; a place where we could stay away from people and beings like you. Kalean, you are not superior, just strong willed. I can and will stop that; I will take all you have if you persist in the destruction of this man and his crew. You see, Kalean, we—my queen and I—moved my world ninety billion light-years away over three hundred years ago.

Kalean shouted, "You lie, that is impossible! No one can travel that far or live that long."

Zin said, "Yet, here we are." "Lies, all lies!" Kalean shouted. Zin started to say something when his queen took him by the arm. "My husband does not lie." Kalean sat in silence, looking around at the strange being he had met. Kalean looked at Zin. "This is another sign of your weakness—you let females speak."

Tressa said, "As the wife and queen of Boldlygo, I assure you I will speak when I please. It is you who has no respect." Tressa raised her hand, stretched forward, and Kalean went against the wall. I choked back a smile.

Zin said to me, "Paxton, I have been informed your ship is repaired and ready to deploy when you are."

Cavota said, "Tomorrow, then." I was glad to be leaving. I was thankful for all Cavota had done for me; I told him I would see that he was reimbursed for his time. Cavota waved his hand to say forget it.

Walking to the hanger to inspect my ship, Zin said to me: "Paxton, I have been to your world. I was much younger. I saw your world was as mine. It is a tropical world; Boldlygo is, too." The others that came with Zin talked amongst themselves. The one called Adair asked Zin: "You think we could take him home for a while? You can bring that bag of shit Kalean, too. Just so we can keep an eye on him. If we leave him here, he could destroy Paxton's ship."

Zin smiled, "Adair, I have something waiting on Kalean if he persists in destroying Paxton's ship." Cavota told Zin he could place Kalean in one of the cells in the prison. Smiles were exchanged.

Tressa and Adair took Leah's hand and walked to the place where they appeared. A blueish gray light appeared as the wall opened. I stood in completely amazement. Zin had his arms extended while I looked at another world—a world like no other. It was like a mystical world.

Leah said, "You're right, Paxton—we have unicorns and Pegasus." Leah laughed out loud as I stood in disbelief. The girls stepped through the hole as we followed. From one world to another, millions of miles into space or farther. Zin told me it takes three months to travel from the moon to home by ship. Here, we did this in seconds.

I could not believe this place. What I was seeing overlooking the valley was—well, I have never seen such. Kalean staggered as he demanded to know what kind of magic this was. "You have placed me in a trance. Release me now."

Cavuto said, "Kalean, I asked you before you came here if your people could do this. You never answered. You only said you were the superior race and we were weak. Kalean never said another word."

I walked to a huge open doorway looking over what seemed to go forever. I could see the tops of buildings below.

Walking closer to the edge that was separated by a wall, I looked over and it must have been a thousand feet down. The valley was a luscious green. To the east of the valley was a herd of a special kind of animal. Leah and Tressa walked up and saw the look on my face.

Leah said, "Paxton, I told you we had them." I told them I have never seen one before; my father told me of them, yet I was skeptical. You know, my world of Ticoru is a beautiful place—from the ice caps to the tropical valleys—but this place was mystical. The girls called Zin; they told him they were going to the city. I was asked to join them. I looked at Kalean; Zin replied, "Do not think of him; he will be fine." Tressa had him in a glow of some kind. I tell you I have never experienced anything like this before.

I thought my mother had power; she could see things sometimes before they happened. Her power was nothing compared to what I have experienced since I have been with Cavota.

Basco ask if I would join him at the lad? I felt compelled to go. Walking into the lad, it was a superb building, unlike any I have never seen. A younger male was working on a project. Looking up he smiled and spoke, "Hello, Paxton."

Right away I asked, "How do you know my name?" A female stood beside him. "Paxton, this is my son, Brinks. Brinks can read mind thoughts. It is a natural thing here on the planet for some." Then it occurred to me: thinking, I smiled. Brinks replied, "Paxton, you will be here as long as it takes." Brinks saying that—well, I was going to enjoy the stay if I could. Walking away, I joined Basco and Adair.

Walking down the path to the city, I must admit it was a beautiful city, with a waterfall along the way and a stream rushing into a beautiful park. Simply fantastic.

Basco asked me of my world. I told him, as well as the others, as much as I could. I told them of the ice caps of the mountains of Ticoru. Leah and Adair said they remember snow and ice on earth. We sat for several hours talking; the conversation we had was an intelligent one; from home to here on this wonderful planet, these people were wise.

Several people stopped by and Basco introduced me to them. Most nodded; others said it was a pleasure. Dorn joined us. I must say he was someone I wished to speak with. Dorn mention several people, and Fina and Shila were two I also wanted to meet. Dorn said they lived on their world of Galaxo. I knew I would be leaving soon and I wanted to see them—I had heard so much of their travels.

For the next few hours, we talked about different things. I ask Dorn of earth.

Dorn said, "Tell me Paxton, what would you like to know? First, you are human, so you do not need to worry—the earth people will accept you." I looked at Dorn with a look of, "What do you mean?"

Dorn said, "Look Paxton, humans on earth destroy what they do not understand. You see, there are no beings like us on earth. You see the natives here walking around—if the

2 4

humans on earth saw them, they would kill them or put them in the government places and do experiments on them. You see, Paxton, there are no aliens—as they call them—past the Milky Way. You will see what I mean, yet they call us uncivilized."

I said, "Dorn, you are human." Well, Dorn showed me his true self; I almost showed him mine. Shaking my head to bring myself back to reality, everyone was laughing.

Time comes and goes. We returned to the palace to wait for Zin. I tell you I was loving everything about this place; I only hoped that someday I might return to extend my stay.

Zin sent a sentry to me with a message. The message said there is someone you should meet. I told the sentry I would come to the pad. "Tell Zin I will meet him there." A woman stopped and called to me. "Paxton, come this way. Zin is not at the pad." I asked, "Who are you?"

She replied, "I am Shasta. The person Zin wanted you to meet is not coming by ship, silly."

"Them how is she coming?" I asked. Then I remembered the portal—walking to the chambers with Shasta, the portal opened. Two beautiful young women stood and Zin introduced them—it was Shila and Fina. They made their way to Tressa and she took their hands while smiling at me. Shasta said, "Oh my, Fina and the bitch." I thought Fina would chock. Fina said, "Well, Shasta, I see you have not forgotten her name." Adair and the other girls laughed out loud. Tressa's mother and father were laughing, too. I was introduced to all. For some reason they treated me as a family member; I was not sure why, as it was my first time here.

The day passed on as we made our way for the evening meal. Let me tell you this was an experience for me—I have never seen so many different things on a table. It was great. There was food here and I had no idea what it was, so I tried all of it. Big mistake—I was so full I could not move. I wondered how long before I would leave, yet I did not want to leave; I could learn to love this place; love these people—but I do not belong here.

Shila told me her and Fina lived on Galaxo. "Maybe someday you could come to our world." I told her I would love to. I talked to everyone here—I do mean everyone. Fina told me her father was the king of the Claxtons. I had to ask. Fina said, "Claxtons are my species. We are not humans like you." Shila said with a smile, "Paxton the bitch has pointed ears." Well, I saw Fina making her way to Shila. She grabbed her as they went rolling to the floor; they rolled into Basco. Again, everyone laughed out loud which made me love these people more. I looked at King Kar; he was smiling and saying, "Will you two ever grow up?" Kar give his approval to come to Galaxo anytime.

My thoughts went to Kalean; I wondered if he was still in whatever that was Tressa placed him in. What was his intentions after we leave here? I feel—no, I know—he will try and destroy my ship.

The last person I spoke to before leaving was Leah. I asked her where on earth she was from. She told me in a conversation that she was from a place called Russia. She also told me of Shila and Fina's trip there. She said they were in a sprit body, then on a ship. I looked at her to say, "What?" Leah laughed.

Leah and I talked long before Zin said it was time to go. Standing, I told him I was not ready, yet I knew we must leave. I stopped by the chambers to tell everyone it was a pleasure to meet them. I said hopefully we can meet again; I told them they were lucky to have a home as beautiful as Boldlygo. I also told them it was nice to be treated as one of the family. Ellie's husband mi told me to stop again.

I replied, "I would really love that. Maybe on my way back from earth's galaxy." Zin told me I should be safe. Looking at him with a smile, my mind went to Kalean.

I will never understand how someone could control or have this much control over their brain. What does it take? I will never know. Zin opened the portal as we stepped through to the moon of spores, walking into the courtyard as if we never left. Cavota waited as the portal closed behind us. I looked around to make sure I was alive or awake; I was not sure. Looking to see Kalean, I knew I was alive— Kalean was pissed.

Zin had Tressa drop the shield or glow as it was from Kalean; he dropped to the ground shouting. I stood watching as he made his way to a standing position. Zin sat on a small wall waiting for Kalean to gain his balance.

Kalean said, "You have no right to do this to me."

Zin smiled, "I did nothing to you; my queen does not like you. She wanted to place you in prison here. I would suggest you be silent, sir." Kalean started to speak, looking down as the orange glow started to cover his feet. Kalean yelled, "Stop please, just let me go. Let me go to my ship; I will leave."

Zin stood from the small wall. "Yes Kalean, you will leave. Kalean, if you attack Paxton's ship again, I will destroy you. You have seen what I can do—believe me I will be watching you. I will destroy the ship and your crew—everything you have."

Kalean replied, "You would not dare."

Zin said, "Do not try me. Kalean, wherever you go, I or Tressa will see. You cannot hide from us." Two sentries walked down the ramp of the ship. Since Kalean had not fully regained his legs, they helped him board the ship. I knew in my heart it was not over, and I said as much. Zin told me to continue my journey. "Paxton, when you return, come to my world."

Standing in the courtyard on the moon, we watched Kalean's ship fade into the distance of the atmosphere. I smiled at Zin, "Do you think Kalean has had enough?"

Zin said, "What do you think, Paxton?" Replying, I told Zin I believe Kalean will destroy me, my ship, and my crew before I reach the blue planet of earth.

From the time I was here on the moon, spending so much time with Cavota, I have found a good friend within him and King Zin. In the brief time, I have found a family in space. When the morning light came to the sky, I would continue my journey to earth.

Leaving the moon, Cavota told me to stay on course if possible. "Follow the star charts. There are a few planets and a few moons—stay away from the Star of Joni; the beings there do not like humans, except for a few. From here, the next place you will find is the Moon of Corning. If you stop, I suggest you do it is a four-month journey. You will find Redda, a good man; he will give you the latest on what is happening in the universe."

CHAPTER 5

THE MORNING STARTED AS ALWAYS. I WOKE UP from a dream and lay on the bed looking into the mirror. I was a young woman waiting on something, yet I knew not what it was. Many thoughts ran through my mind. Why am I having these dreams, I ask myself? It was as if I was trying to reach out to something or someone that was not there. It could be someone was trying to call me—it was so real, like they were there in my dreams, if there was such a place. It was just bits and pieces. I do not belong here, yet I am here. Where else would I be? I have lived in Russia all my life.

My mother told me once there were no pictures of my ancestors until the late 1800s. This I found confusing—there were no images of anyone. In my thoughts, how besides writings do we know who they were? I suppose I will have to be content to believe the writings. The photos I have did not belong here on earth. Smiling, I thought maybe they belonged somewhere beyond the stars.

I have a small book that was passed down to me, from a distant relative. I find myself reading it often. To think some of them lived that long ago—I cannot tell you who I am or where I am from. I do remember my mother telling me someday I would find my way. I still do not understand what she meant. Find my way where? Where was I going; how was I going; how was I to get there—I thought where was there? In my thought there were so many questions unanswered.

This morning would be no different than any other; I would start by dressing for school. I noticed in the mirror my body had begun to fill out more. I would soon be sixteen; I was already bigger than most of the girls here. I liked the way I was beginning to fill out.

My thoughts went back to the dream I had in the night. I began having these dreams when I was younger, I think. The more I have these dreams, the more intense they become; I more I dream, the more real they become. There was not much I had in my life to hold on to—my father, I never knew; my mother passed away when I was younger. So, I have been alone since.

I remember on several occasions, I would be gazing into the heavens and stars. It appeared she was looking for someone or something. It was as in my dreams—who was this girl I dreamed about named Hannah? I know no one named

Hannah, yet I dream of her. Could she be a relative or an ancestor?

The morning light had come to the window; I could only make out the gray shadows of the trees. My school-marm called to me from the door as the knock came. Trust me—she was another story. I was still confused as to why she took me in; this woman was incredibly intelligent. I do not know why she was in the position she was in. I believe she could rule the world if she had the chance. Whenever I would tell her this, Sophia would laugh out loud. Sophia would say, "Oh Mimi, you are so funny!" It was like she did not belong here. I need to talk to her one on one—you know, in a place of solitude. I have so many questions. I feel she could answer them—well hopefully, anyway; I feel it would be worth a try.

Knocking again, I told her the door was open. "I am awake; you may enter if you like." Opening the door, she looked at me with eyes as blue as mine. "Dreaming again, Mimi?"

I said, "Always, Sophia."

Sophia replied, "Dream tonight Mimi—time for school. I will meet you downstairs shortly." Sophia was smiling as she walked out the door, leaving another problem behind her—Nina.

Nina was lurking in the hallway. She gazed into my room. I was not sure what she hoped to see; I was fully dressed. This girl was the same age as me, yet Nina was evil—pure evil. I could feel this each time she looked at me; it would always give me chills. I did not like her for some reason; it was a gut feeling. Just as me, she did not belong here.

Today, Sophia said we were going back in time—only in our studies, not in life. I could only wish for that. I loved history; it was a subject I could never get enough of. There were fifteen girls sitting in class talking when Sophia called us to order.

"Today, class, we will be studying other planets and possible life there, if you can believe that." I thought I have heard of this, yet I have seen no proof. Hundreds of years ago here in Russia, history says a spaceship came from the heavens with humanoid beings. It was said they fought the Russian army and defeated them—fact or fiction, yet it is written. There were many sightings of ships. In this small book I have, it speaks of the time. The book is all I have of my ancestors, whoever they were. Someday I will face this as my mother said I would; today I will listen to Sophia.

Nina sat beside me, mumbling something that was not compared to the class. "Nina," I said, "If you are not interested in learning, please be quiet so I can." Nina looked at me with a death look—I kind of got a chill. What the hell, I thought. Nina will kill me.

Nina whispered, "You are a freaking little bitch." It was the first time anyone has ever called me a name like that.

Sophia called out, "Girls, something you would like to share with the rest of the class?" I said nothing.

Nina replied, "No, Sophia; it is just your little pet is a freak."

Walking to the front of the class Sophia said, "Nina, if you wish not to attend this class, you may leave." Looking at Nina with a very strange look, Sophia said, "Nina, I have no pets; if you wish to stay please be respectful to the other students."

"Whatever," Nina answered.

Sophia continued to speak. Sophia said she would be going home this weekend; next week there will be no classes for the week.

Well, this made me incredibly happy, since Nina would be going home. I would be left here at the school alone—well, at least I thought I would be. Sophia released the class. "Go outside and enjoy the sun!" After all, it was an enjoyable day out. I stood from my desk, and I had this feeling come over me; a feeling I have never had before. I staggered, and the class laughed out loud. What was happening to me? Looking at Sophia, it was hard to focus. Everything behind her was turning blue—blue as the sky outside the window.

I screamed, "Sophia!" That was all I remembered. Six hours had passed; I woke up looking at the wall. I was in my room in my bed. Sophia was sitting in a chair reading a book. She was so into the book she did not notice I was awake. Moving my hand, Sophia smiled. "Well, I see you are back. Did you dream again."

My eyes teared up. Tears ran down my cheek. I was choked up. "Sophia, what is wrong with me? Something is wrong. I feel different; strange. Sophia, maybe I am a freak as Nina says. Maybe Nina will kill me, Sophia. If you know anything, please tell me. I do not wish to be like this." Sophia never said a word. Sitting beside my bed looking at me, she sat there as if she was in a trance or something. Sophia said as she stood walked to the window, "Mimi, I cannot say what is happening to you. Maybe it is as your mother said; maybe you are finding your way."

With a puzzled look, I said, "What?"

"Sophia, how could you possibly know what my mother said? I have been with you for six years. Ever since you took me in—you leave to go home and I stay here. Before that, I never knew you; you did not know me, yet here we are."

Sophia said, "Mimi, you will come home with me; maybe we can sort this mystery out. Mimi, do not ever let me hear you call yourself a freak again—you are simply different." Thinking to myself, I knew she was right—I was different. I was about to find out just how different I was. Oh, believe me, it was coming. I could feel it; like the wind that blows, I felt a change coming. This change was coming to my soul, my body, and my mind. How did she know what I was thinking?

Leaving my room Sophia said, "Mimi, this change coming to you—be ready, be prepared; keep an open mind. I will tell you more when we arrive at Moscow." Sophia said goodbye to the other girls. Sophia told me to pack a few things, only clothes. I have plenty where we're going. An hour passed and Sophia asked if I was ready.

The ride did not take long; the school was in the village of Khimki. I have lived in Russia all my life, with several years in Moscow before Sophia found me in a home. I was not sure how she did this. I was the only student at the school she treated like a daughter Sophia made sure I had food, clothes, and learned in my classes. She made sure I listened to what she said. She has said to me more times than I could count: "Mimi, only one thing is more important than education—more education."

Riding along the freeway, looking at the sun as it disappeared behind the mountains, I looked at Sophia and thought she had to be the most intelligent person I could ever meet—that would also prove to be wrong. I thought, Sophia does not belong here. Hell, sometimes I thought that of myself.

CHAPTER 6

SOPHIA HAD THE MUSIC PLAYING; IT WAS AN OLD song, Sophia said. I have heard it before. Tonight, it was a different sound—same song, same words—just sounded strange. I had a very strange feeling coming over me. The song was titled, "I Do Not Belong Here." What was even stranger was the two girls that sang the song were named Josey and Mimi. I never said a word, just smiled. This song was incredibly old, yet it described me—it was as the song says: I do not belong here.

Passing through the rim of Moscow, I noticed a familiar place. I lived in Moscow once when I was small, yet I have never been here. Gazing out the window I said to Sophia, "You missed your turn." Why did I say that? Sophia turned to look at me, smiling.

I ask, "What just happened?" Sophia never said a word. She turned at the next street, coming back to the street we just passed. Sophia stopped at a big house on the street; the walk must have been fifteen steps. Somewhere in a daze, I went out like a candle in the wind.

Waking up in a huge room with sunlight all around, I thought, how did I get here? Where was here? I checked under the cover. I was in a pair of pajamas. Oh my, how did…who did…change my clothes? I hope they enjoyed it, because I was pissed. Whatever is happening to me needs to stop. From a room I took to be the front of the house I could hear voices. I stepped to the door. The sun filled the room through a huge window; it covered the whole wall. I went back to bed and sat there for a moment. The laughter was loud, from a woman's voice I have never heard before and a man—who were these people? I started to stand, but I fell back on the bed. What the hell? I thought. What was wrong with me? I waited a moment then stood. Walking to the sun filled room I stood in the doorway. I could see Sophia having a conversation with an old woman and a young man— thirty years, I would say. Who were these people, and who was Sophia? I have many questions I; will they have the answers I look for?

I decided to try and keep a journal of the time I was here. The next five days were a challenge. The brief time I have been here, things has already started to happen.

DAY ONE

Sophia turned to see me in the doorway. Standing, she smiled at me, making a motion with her hand to enter. Sophia called me by name. "Mimi, come in please." I then entered the room where she and a man stood smiling. He give me a nod with his head, saying hello with a heavy Russian accent, "Young lady, are you feeling better?" Sophia held out her hand. "Come Mimi; I want to introduce you to Ivan."

I was getting that deja vu feeling again. I cannot explain it—it was like I knew him, yet I have—or at least I do not remember—meeting him. Looking at the old woman in the big chair, Sophia said she was Aunt Tasha. Sophia told me in the weeks to come we would spend quite a lot of time together. "Mimi, I promise you will learn from this. Aunt Tasha is highly intelligent. She will help you with your dreams."

I thought, how did she know about my dreams? I promise. I kept this in—the only person I have ever told of this was Sophia. For a girl that was sixteen, I was ready to learn anything I could; I did not know it was about to get crazy. I knew nothing but bits and pieces of my ancestors, and little about my past. I do not believe you can see the future—or can you? Regardless of what ever was going on in my brain, life was going to be different after today.

Tasha did not say much the first day I met her; she just looked at me and listened to me while looking out that big ass window. I have seen big windows before, but not like this one—it covered the whole wall. In my thoughts, I would say she was eighty years old; I have never seen or met anyone that old. She, as Sophia said, had a head full of knowledge—how she gained this, I cannot say. I only knew one thing: she sat looking through that big window. It made me think: what is she looking for? I was not sure, yet maybe she had already seen it. Tasha sat listening to me until the late evening. Sophia came in smiling as always.

Sophia asked, "Mimi, did you have a good day?"

I replied by saying, "Yes, I suppose I did. We—Tasha and I—just talked of school. That was about it." Sophia told me she had things to do in the village and would go again tomorrow. Sophia asked if I would help with dinner. By the time we ate it, was later than I liked. I helped with the dishes, then excused myself to my room.

DAY TWO

I thought I would lie on the bed before I changed into my sleeping attire. Closing my eyes, my thoughts went back to the school. I thought of Nina. I was not sure why I was afraid of her; yet I was. She has called me a freak more than once. Nina said to me I need to die.

Sophia introduced me to Nina on the first day she brought me to the school. I had met Sophia on many occasions when she would come to the home I was at. I noticed Sophia took an interest in me; she come several times to see me, and I was not sure why. The last time she came, I was called in the room with the caretaker. Sophia ask me if I would like to leave this place.

I asked her, "Where would I go? I have no parents; I am alone."

Sophia smiled, "Well, not after today, Mimi." That is how we met. My thoughts went back to Nina. Since that day, every time I see Nina I feel uneasy; nothing has changed. I needed to get away. When Sophia invited me to come here, I took the invitation right away. In the days to come, I will find out more about myself than I already know. I would find out the reason Sophia took to me. Since I was ten years old, I have felt a deep closeness to—I really cannot explain it. Somewhere in the night, I fell asleep.

DAY THREE

The sunshine pierced the morning sky as the rays of light came through my window. Raising up to the side of the bed I thought: well, that was a short night. I slept through without dreaming, which was different. I took a shower and went downstairs. Walking into the kitchen, I poured a cup of tea. It appeared I was the only one up. Walking to the sofa in the great room where Tasha sat, I sat in a chair next to hers. I sat my tea on the table after taking a sip. My thoughts went wild, I suppose; I was not sure how long I had been there when Sophia called me. I took my tea and took a sip—it was cold. I went to the kitchen and took a sweet cake and was sitting at the table when Sophia walked to me.

Sophia said, "Come with me Mimi, Aunt Tasha would like to talk to you. Mimi, I must go into the village—this will give you and Aunt Tasha the chance to talk. Mimi remember this: keep an open mind—you must."

I was on edge. Looking at Sophia, I said, "I do not understand, Sophia. Why do I need to do that?"

Sophia said, "Mimi, before we leave on Sunday, you will see thing at a different level; this I promise." I told Sophia I just want the dreams to stop—the dreams of someone named Hannah. I do not know who this person could be; I do not know her. Sophia said, as she smiled and walked to the door, "Open mind Mimi; open mind." Sophia walked through the door. I found out before Sophia returned that Tasha loved to talk and she was intelligent.

Sophia led the way to the big window where Tasha was sitting. Approaching her I thought, does this woman ever sleep? She was holding out her hands and smiling.

Tasha said, "Come closer, Mimi; let me look at you." She acted as if she knew me all my life. I knew this could not be true, because I have never met or heard of her.

Tasha said, "Mimi, you do not know me, yet before this day is over you will see me in an unusual way. Sophia told you to keep an open mind."

Looking at Tasha I said, "Yes, she did. I am not sure why I need to do that, but I will try."

Tasha said, "Mimi, life is what we make it. I want to tell you a story if you will listen." I told her I would listen; this is where I needed to keep an open mind.

Tasha replied, "Mimi, you should always keep an open mind. You never know what you might run into." I told her that is what I am afraid of; "You see, Tasha, with an open mind trouble, could overtake you."

Tasha started her story about a long time ago. I took a sip of my tea and thought this is going to be quite a story.

I settled back, pulled my legs under me, and listened to Tasha talk. Tasha was speaking of people whom I have never heard; I had no clue who they were. She talked of a few people I read about in the small books I have, books that were passed down from others. I sat listening to her for over an hour. I stopped her to go to the bathroom. I stopped by my room and took a small book from my bag. Flipping through the pages I found the name—Ira. In the writing, this man played an important part in the history of our people. I went back to the great room, gave the book to Tasha, where she took the book and looked carefully at the worn pages. Then, she looked at me.

Tasha asked, "Mimi, where did you get this?" I told her my mother gave it to me. "My mother told me it was from our ancestors. Tasha, I am not sure where she got it. She only told me it was passed down from our family. She told me to keep it, that someday I would find where I need to be.

It is my belief that it starts here; this I cannot be sure of. I only know it has no bearing on my dreams."

Tasha smiled, "Mimi, your dreams—Sophia told me about them. I promise we will get to that; let me finish my story."

I sat and listened to Tasha most of the day—the old woman could talk. The story she told was so real. She told her story with feeling; it was as if you were there. My thoughts went to Sophia; she had been gone for hours. I was beginning to wonder about her. When she did return, she was smiling, as always.

Smiling, Sophia asked," "Learning anything, Mimi?" I never said a word; I just looked at her. Tasha took my hand; she told me we will talk again.

I said, "Yes we will, lady." I embraced Sophia—why, I was not sure. I did not know if I was glad to see her or the fact I was glad that she returned. I excused myself to my room. Walking to the window I thought; where did the day go? I could see the day had ended. The sun had started its descent to the far mountain to the west; night was coming again to Moscow. I thought as I sat on the edge of the bed, where had Sophia been? Where did she go? Maybe she has a man in her life—this I was not sure of. Sophia spent all her time with the girls at the school. If she was not with me, she was with another girl. Then a thought come to me: why was I here? It did not make sense to me, yet here I was.

Opening the door, I walked to the small porch. A cool, gentle breeze stirred the night air. Looking up, I saw what appeared to be a star shoot across the dark sky. I could feel snow in the air. If anyone lived their life in Russia you learned that when the air cooled; snow was in the future. From the small porch, I heard a voice behind me. Turning, I saw it was Sophia. I stepped through the door to greet her.

I asked Sophia, "Where have you been all day?" Of course there was no reply.

"Sophia, I asked you a question. Where have you been?"

Sophia replied, "Mimi, I do not have to answer you. You did ask, so I will tell you. Mimi, it was one of the reasons I wanted to come home. I had an appointment with my doctor."

My heart raced. "Sophia, are you sick?" I asked with a lump in my throat. She told me she was fine. How could I be sure of what she said? Sophia and I talked for a while. I told her of the day spent with Tasha and the story she told. Sophia said Tasha had told her the same story when she was about my age. Sophia told me Tasha was old. She said if Tasha knew Mayrra was alive, she would pass.

"Sophia, who is Mayrra?" I asked.

Sophia said, "Mayrra left here long ago, Mimi. The thought of her returning is what keeps her going—Tasha should be dead. Mayrra was fifteen when she left; by now she would be thirty earth years. Mayrra was Tasha's grand-daughter." I looked skeptically at Sophia.

"Earth years. Sophia, what the hell does that mean?" I asked. Sophia smiled, leaving the room. "You soon will find out my dear little friend; you will soon find out." I took a shower and changed to my sleeping clothes. I walked to the big window in the front room. Tasha was talking to Ivan and Sophia. Ivan never said much. I told them I was going to bed. Sophia told me she would see me in the morning. Lying in my bed, I thought of today's event—it had been a long one. Somewhere in the night, I fell asleep.

DAY FOUR

Time comes and goes. The thing about time is it waits on no one—time does not have to. The warmth of the morning sun through the bedroom window woke me. I was thinking of the previous night's event. Sophia told me she could not answer some of my questions; she told me that would be for Tasha to answer. She did tell me before we go back to school that all my questions would be answered. "If not, there would be another time—just try to spend as much time with Tasha as you can. After all, Mimi, you do not need to sight see; you were born in Russia." Sophia said this as she left the room. For some reason, there was more to what was going on here. Did I want to know? I was not sure.

Thoughts of school came to mind. It was not the thought of returning to school that I feared—it was Nina. I could not understand why this girl did not like me. Maybe in another life I wronged her; this I do not believe; I believe in here and now; I believe in tomorrow. Maybe I will ask Tasha—maybe she will have an answer.

Maybe I am a freak; maybe I do not belong here. I thought, maybe I should run. In my heart, that is not possible for me. Now, why did I think that? Since I have been in this school, Nina has been a complete bitch to me—I mean a real bitch. I know I do not wish to deal with her. Hell, maybe I should run.

Moving from my bed to the window, I caught a glimpse of something. Looking closer, it was Sophia. What was she doing? I placed my robe around myself and walked to the front room. Sophia came through the door.

"Good morning, Mimi; sleep well?" Sophia asked.

I replied, smiling, "You really want to know, or just being polite, Sophia?" Sophia walked to me, placing her hand on my chest. Sophia pushed me hard—she me back to the wall.

Sophia said in a muffled voice, "Listen, you little ass." Then she backed up. Damn, I thought, she was going to hurt me. Sophia said, "Go change your clothes; come for breakfast."

I was shaking all over. I have never pictured Sophia as a violent person. Today, I saw a different person. I was not sure what was going on in the brain; I only know I did not like it. I ran to my room, closing the door behind me. I stood with my back against the door and took a deep breath as tears ran down my cheeks. I had no idea at the time that she was only goofing around.

I pulled my thoughts together and changed into a pair of jeans and a long sleeve shirt. The morning was cool outside and I was going to take a walk down the street after breakfast. Snow was coming and you could feel it in the air. From the great room where Tasha sat in front of that big window I could hear the sound of music—it was playing that old song again; the one I have learned to love. I do not belong here.

I walked cautiously to the dining area. I truly did not know what to expect. Tasha was in her usual place. Sophia came in with a bowl of scrambled eggs and potatoes. I loved the way she cooked them with onions. Sophia smiled as she passed them to me. My throat had a lump in it as I said thank you. Sophia looked at me with a strange look, as if to say what is wrong? I never said a word.

Tasha broke the silence by saying: "Mimi, after your walk, today will be different. You have been here three days listening to me tell my stories. Today, there will be no stories. You will be going back to school in three days. Mimi, for the next three days, I will only talk to you if you ask questions. Sophia said you have quite a few. Remember: have an open mind when I answer them. Sophia and I will answer them. Mimi, you will hear things you won't believe, yet all are true." I did not know what to think. Tasha reached out, took my hand, and led me to the great room. The sun was so warm shining through the window; the leather on the chair even felt warm.

Tasha smiled, "Mimi, hidden somewhere inside of you is a power; with the help of Sophia, you must find this power." Tasha sat quietly for a moment. "Mimi, remember: keep an open mind. Sophia is strong with her power. With the power hidden inside of you, you will be able to call to the family with your mind. Believe me, Mimi—they will come—only if you can control the power within." I swallowed hard, looking at Sophia.

Sophia said, "It is true Mimi—we can do this; it's what must be done."

My heart was beating so fast I was having problems breathing. I could not believe what I was hearing. I jumped from the table. "I am not a freak," I was screaming. Tasha held out her hand, "Mimi, please, you must have an open mind."

"Tasha please, I understand having an open mind, but what you are saying is not possible." After calming down, I sat and tried to eat. There were many thoughts running through my mind. One thought kept returning time after time—what have I gotten myself into. A huge, strange house; an old woman; a teacher I knew nothing about, except the fact that she took me in. I had no complaint of the way Sophia has taken care of me; what I did have a problem with is what they were saying.

I sat listening to Sophia and Tasha speak in Russian; I suppose it was easier than English. I could speak some Russian, yet I prefer English. Everyone in Russia spoke English. Maybe it was the fact everything was in English. I asked Sophia if I could help clear the table. I do believe she knew what was on my thoughts, so Sophia told me to go for my walk. I almost ran from the room. I took a sweater, since it was cool out, and left the house. Twenty minutes later, I returned.

Entering the house through the great room, I walked fast to my room. Tasha and Sophia sat talking. I went to my room to the dresser. I opened a drawer and took out a book that Tasha gave me of someone—the book was written in Russian and broken English now and then. I found what I was looking for; Tasha wrote this and she wanted me to see this.

"My beloved Mayrra left me today. In my heart, I hope to meet her again. Mayrra, accompanied with Valdimir, Sara, Michel, Jacob—descendants of the earth family—are going to the United States, to a place called New Mexico." I paused; I remembered Sophia speaking of Mayrra—if she went to the America, why has she not returned? The reading says she has been gone for over fifteen years. Sophia also said she was one year younger than me when she left. Why did she leave and where was she now? Why did she not come back?

I was writing things down when Sophia called to me; walking to the door, Sophia looked at me. I could read her thoughts. I said, "Tell Tasha I will be there; let me make my bed first." Sophia smiled, "Why did you say that? How did you know what I was going to say?" I told her I was not sure. I made my bed, gathered my writing, and went to the great room. Tasha was facing the window, as she always had in the few days I have been here.

I asked, "Tasha, do you ever sleep?" Smiling, Tasha said, "Sit, Mimi." Taking a chair, Tasha told me to pull it closer. Tasha started by saying, "Mimi, my people do not need much sleep." I was looking for Sophia and she called from the kitchen, "I will be there, Mimi." Now I ask myself, how did she know I was looking for her? I could not explain it; this shit was getting stranger every minute.

Tasha began her story. "Mimi, hundreds of years ago, a being came to earth from the stars."

I shook my head hard and replied, "What?" Tasha held out her hand, "Let me finish, Mimi." Tasha started again as Sophia come into the room. Walking to the sofa, Sophia sat down, looking at me and smiling. Tasha said again, "From the stars, Mimi. According to our history, it was not his first time here. Mimi, I assure you it was not the last. They have visited us hundreds of times. Some of our people wrote it down, some like in this book of yours. Bota was his name; there were others. Bota was the first of our people, and Shila was the last. It has been many years since she was here; she took my Mayrra home. I sent the other children with her. Mimi, what some do not understand is that this power is combined in our DNA, and it is special. Most of us have powers but only females. The males did have some powers, like Ira—most do not know this; some do not care. Then some never find this out.

Mayrra could manipulate people; she could do this just by touch. I was told once they could change into other people just by touching them. Mimi, after today you will see things in an unusual way, I promise you this." Little did Tasha know, I already did.

"In the beginning of our earth family, a female was brought to earth—her name was Destiny. That was a long time ago. Repeatedly, he would return. Destiny had a child, from what was called a DNA transfer. This DNA was from Mya. Mya was a princess of the planet; her father was Maoke. Maoke was the ruler of the planet we call Boldygo. Over the years, Bota would return and he would always bring a scientist with him. Bota would let this being do this DNA transfer on one of the females, if she were of age. Believe me Bota, could have done this himself, yet Bota was a pilot and a shipwright, and he also was a great scientist."

I sat listening with my mouth open. Sophia would say, "Close your mouth, Mimi; a fly is going to fly in." I listened to this and shook my head—I could not believe what Tasha was saying.

I asked Tasha, "Who are you referring to? I do not know these people; and what is Boldlygo or whatever you said?"

I said, "So it would appear we are descendants of royal blood." I said this out loud. Tasha agreed.

Standing, I walked around the table not saying a word; just looking. Sophia could see the look I had. I said, "This, it's total bullshit. This is ludicrous. You said keep an open mind. If someone believed this shit, they would not have a mind."

Sophia stood and stretched out her arm as a damn pillow flew across the room, hitting the wall beside me. Well guess what—yes, my mouth was open again! That was it, I flew into my room screaming for help. I was in shock. With my back against the wall, I slid to a sitting position. Placing my hands across my knees, I laid my head across my arms. I swear I was shaking like on a tree in a gentle breeze. Ten minutes later, I was still calling for someone to help me. My head was lying on my knees when the door unlocked. Looking up stood a man—it was Ivan. Ivan was the man I saw when I arrived and once again in the living room. Ivan stared at me; I was the color of the clouds. "Mimi, I am Ivan."

I replied, "I know who you are. I met you when I first got here. "

Ivan said, "Mimi, listen to what Aunt Tasha and Sophia says. I assure you all of what they say is true. Sophia over the years has become powerful with her power. Believe me, Mimi, she can do other things, too."

I looked at Ivan, "Please do not hurt me."

Ivan said, "Hurt you? Mimi, why would you say this? You are my family. I promise, no one is going to hurt you or do anything to you. Sophia is your aunt, your father's sister. There were not a lot of males born to our family. Your father and I are the last; I am your uncle. Tasha and Sophia thought it would be best not to tell you until we had this talk. I know you are frightened; I would be, too."

I tried to stand with my back against the wall. I was crying and shaking; I could not stand still. Sophia came into the room looking at me. I cried out to her. "Oh, Sophia, help me please." Sophia ran to me and took me in her arms.

Sophia said, "I am sorry, Mimi. It was not my place to tell you. Aunt Tasha and I, along with Ivan, thought it would be best. Besides, Aunt Tasha wanted to be the one to tell you. I promise we are the last of the earth family. Mimi, we spent a long time looking for you. When Mayrra left, Tasha called to me. You were only two years old when Mayrra left, and your mother was never around us much. When she passed, Tasha was called. The Russian government placed you in a care facility. We looked and looked until that day I found you. I brought you here, then to the school."

I asked, "What do you mean I am the last?"

Ivan said, "The last of our people of earth. Mimi, hundreds of years ago, Destiny started our family on earth, and it ends with you. Our lives started on a farm, not far from here. Generations of people—some here in Russia, some in England, some in the America, and some in Spain. I am so glad it is over; I want to leave. Tasha and Sophia said if you call, Hannah will hear you."

"Hannah." I said. "How the hell do you know about Hannah?"

Ivan replied, "Mimi please, if you call her, she will hear you."

I said, "My ass I will, I want nothing more to do with this bullshit." I pushed Sophia away; I told her to take me back to school. "Sophia, I would rather deal with Nina."

Sophia said, "Fine, you little bitch." That pissed me off to the point that I turned, slinging my arms all in one motion—then the damn closet door blew into a million pieces.

Sophia said, "Now, Mimi—do you believe me? See what you can do when you are pissed off?" In disbelief, I stood shaking and asked them to leave me alone. Locking the door as they left I said out loud, "Little good that will do."

I walked to my bed and slipped off my shoes. I thought, just for a moment I would lay here; see if I could gather my thoughts—then I drifted off to sleep. Somewhere in my dream, I dreamed again of Hannah. Opening my eyes, I saw that it was dark; I was cold. Looking around, something was strange—I was floating above my bed. I thought, wait, what the hell? I screamed so loud people in Moscow could hear me. I screamed for Sophia or anyone—no one came; I was alone. Then I felt myself settle down on the bed. From somewhere in the room, a voice called. It sounded as if it was coming from the closet that I shattered earlier.

"Who is there?" I asked. "It is I, Mimi—you called to me."

"Bullshit," I said. "If it is you, come into the light." Stepping into the light was the female I had dreamed about throughout the years—she was exactly the way she looked in my dreams.

Hannah said, "Mimi, this is a dream. I promise you we will meet soon. I must go; I need to talk to my king." I thought to myself, yes, bullshit. "Mimi, I am not sure what bullshit is. I will come to you again. I will bring my mother; her name is Shila. Tasha will tell you of Shila. Until then." My eyes opened and I was so scared. I ran from the room through the house, running for the door. Sophia stepped in front of me.

Sophia asked, "Mimi, where are you going?"

I said, "Sophia, please; I have to get the hell out of here."

Sophia asked, "Well, where will you go, Mimi?"

Tasha called to me, "Mimi, come here; talk to me." I tried to talk—I really did. I was so nervous and shaking so badly. I finally calmed down enough to tell them of the night's events. Sometimes when I opened my mouth, a big lump got in my throat. I told Tasha what happened in my room; I told her how I destroyed the closet and then went to sleep and had that dream. Hours had passed before I woke up.

Sophia said, "Mimi, you have only been in your room for twenty minutes."

"Bullshit," Ivan said, "Mimi, tell them." "Like I said, I just want to go back to school." Sophia told me to wait; she would take me back later. I went back to my room and fell asleep.

The morning came early and I was glad. Tasha spent the next two days talking to me. We spent seven days there, in total.. Sophia and I drove back to school without saying much; it had been a long week. When we arrived back to school, I was ready for miss Nina. If that bitch comes close to me, I will beat the shit out of her.

CHAPTER 7

CAVOTA TOLD ME TO GIVE KALEAN TWO DAYS BE-
fore I left. Ships would escort him to the edge of the galaxy.
I enjoyed the moon while I was there—it is a different kind
of place. On the morning of the third day, it was time for
me and my crew to leave. I did hear some of the crew say
they should stay. I admit I have had quite the adventure
since I have arrived here.

Cavota told me to stay away from the Star of Joni.
Filling me in on the journey, he said my next stop should be
the Moon of Corning. "If all is true, in one year you should
reach Saturn. There, you make your turn to earth. Paxton,
always stay on a charted path." Cavota told me that, with
the upgrade that was made to my ship, I could stay stealthily
hidden. "Paxton, never stop or let anyone board you. Follow
these rules and you should be safe."

My crew went aboard the ship. Cavota told us we would be welcome anytime on the moon. One crew member ask if he could live here—Cavota told him it would be an honor to have him. With that said and the engines roaring, my pilot lifted us off into the darkness of space.

Going into the darkness, I was asked "Where to?" I told him to plot a course to the Moon of Corning. Leaving the Moon of Spores behind was almost like leaving home. I had made some dear friends along the way, none like the ones on the moon or like on the planet of Boldlygo. I never made it to Galaxo, I am to say. In my heart I know I will someday. I did, however, meet Shila and Fina. I wanted to meet Shila's daughter and her mate, Jawah. King Icol stepped down; Hannah and Jawah took control of the humans. King Kar was still in control of the Claxton's.

The flight from the Moon of Spores went as good as expected—there was no sighting of Kalean. Yet, I knew somewhere in the vast darkness of space he waited; he was waiting for me. I could feel this as I was alone with my thoughts.

I had left the bridge to be alone for a while. I was studying star charts when the bridge called.

"Captain, come to the bridge, please." I thought as I left my quarters, what now? Entering the bridge, the pilot told me we were entering the moon's airspace.

I said, "Call the moon for landing instruction." It appeared Cavota had relayed the message we would be stopping. Three months in space and I was ready to walk on the ground. Looking at the screen, two ships appeared. My pilot called out, "Captain, we are being held, sir."

I took the transmitter, "I am captain Paxton of the Ticoru ship."

The ship's captain replied, "I know who you are. Do you have a shuttle?" I told him no he told me to follow him. Breaking through the moon's atmosphere, I found this place to be a beautiful place. The city was as modern as they come. I was told to go to the landing pad to the north; it will be marked with the letter P. My pilot did as he was told.

He sat the ship down just like I would have done. We sat waiting for the ramp to lower. Shutting down the engines and opening the hatch, at the bottom stood a big man. I walked down to meet him and his hand stretched out and took mine.

"Greetings from Corning," He spoke. I told him it was a pleasure. He informed me Cavota had called several times. He said you would be gathering your supplies for your journey to earth.

The big man smiled, "I am Redda, governor of the moon. I know who you are. Cavota told me all about you."

"Cavota is an honorable man," I spoke. Redda told me him and Cavota go way back. Redda wanted to know what was going on in the outside world. I told him all I could. I told him I was stranded on the Moon of Spores for weeks; I also told him of my visit to Boldlygo with King Zin. I told him of Shila and Fina, of Leah and Dorn. He was most excited. Redda told me to tell my crew to come ashore. "Do not worry about your ship. No one—I mean no one—will board it. Tell you crew to take leave. I have a list of supplies for you; do not worry, we will bring them to the hanger. Then you may watch them loaded on your ship. Stay if you like, Paxton."

Redda told me, "Cavota said you would give me one stone." As the day was ending, I wanted to go back to the ship. I told the crew to take in the town but that you must return to the ship; all agreed. After the supplies were loaded, I told Redda I would retire for the night and would be leaving early. Redda told me he would see me off. Saying our farewell for the evening, Redda departed and so did I. I told the crew we would be leaving early. Of course, it made no difference, since it was always dark ten minutes after liftoff.

I loved space; there was no end to the vast emptiness and cold darkness. My father told me that once and King Zin told me the same. He told me he moved his planet ninety billion light-years away. It was beyond me to think of such a thing. Zin told me he and Bota researched this for years—they would go into a meditation, before settling where they were before moving back; a moon, an asteroid—yet there were no life. It does make one wonder.

Walking to my quarters and peering through the portal window, I looked at the corning moon. It seemed to hold a message, but I could not say what kind of message. Changing into my night clothes, I laid across the bed. Somewhere in the cool night, I fell asleep.

I was not sure how long I had been asleep when a voice called out to me. Lying still, I raised my head; looking around, I saw nothing—there was no one. Closing my eyes, I fell into a restful sleep just to be wakened again. The voice called. "Paxton, wake up," the voice said. Ok, I thought, this is weird. I had a chill run down my back; I called out: "Who is there?"

"It is I, Paxton," the female voice said. "You do not know me, Paxton."

I asked, "Who are you? Wait, where are you?" The voice said, "Beware; trouble follows." Jumping up, I dressed and ran to the bridge. I called the pilot as I entered. "Is everyone aboard?" He told me all were present and accounted for. I called to the control of the moon and asked to speak to Redda. While waiting for Redda, I told the pilot to prepare to get underway. I explained to Redda what had happened and he told me to lift off. "Paxton, go hard and fast. From the experiences I have faced, listen to the voices. It would appear someone is watching after you."

Looking at the faces of the crew, I could see the looks I was getting. Redda told me to cloak my ship on lift off. "Paxton, you have clearance to leave. Take care; maybe someday we will meet again." I did as instructed and in no time, we were in the darkness of space.

Flying through the atmosphere, the moon appeared to be a tiny ball in space. I hoped we were not seen or picked up on a screen of another ship. Redda said someone was watching; I could not imagine who. However, the voice was female—maybe Leah or Tressa? If it was the people of Boldlygo, then they were extraordinarily strong in mind power.

Leaving the bridge, I walked to the galley. I had a cup of tea and a bread cake. I had never had one until I made my journey to Boldlygo. I also had never had sweetgrass, and it was delightful. Sitting at a table, several of the crew were talking of current events.

I said, "Well, it would appear you liked the moon."

One said, "Captain, our plant of Ticoru is a paradise; the Moon of Spores was a treat. It is a story I will tell forever. If we ever return, I will ask Cavota if I may stay." I told him that would be his wish; I had no way of knowing of his future.

Night and day was hard to distinguish, since it was always dark. It was an awfully awkward thing to adjust to. We did what was expected of us; the crew and I did what we had to do. One month after leaving the moon, a call came from the bridge. Jabel and I were in the engine room; we made our way hastily to find we were entering the Star of Joni's air space. We were in stealth mode as the pilot brought the ship to a full stop.

I asked, "Have we been detected?" I was told, "No, captain." I asked Jabel to come to the star chart. Pointing to it, I asked about the space to the outside of Joni.

Jabel replied, "Dead space, captain. It is uncharted and we do not need to go in; there is no telling what is out there."

Cavota has told me to never travel in uncharted space. There is a reason why, I must agree.

I turned to the bridge, "Well, should we stay cloaked and try?" All agreed. "So be it then; let's go," I said.

Rove made way to the outside of the star; from the planet there was no travel. We watched the scope as we made our way and nothing showed up. Rove was well above the flight path; he was moving faster than I would have liked. Looking on the scope, I wondered what the star was like. Why did most travelers avoid the star? Was it as bidding as Cavota said? Well, Zin seemed to think so. I only knew I wanted no trouble with anyone. In less than an hour, we had cleared the air space of the star.

Time comes and goes; it is hard to keep up with things. I suppose that is why the captain keeps a log. After ten months, we came upon a planet that is shown on the star chart—it was the planet Zin and Tressa destroyed. Well almost—Shila finished it on her crusade. I was told Shila was a furious warrior. She must be; she had the Claxtons behind her.

I told Rove to take us beyond the atmosphere. "Let us see what the planet looks like now." Breaking through the atmosphere at sixty-five thousand feet descending, I could tell that at one time it was a beautiful planet. It had been several years since Shila destroyed it. Flying across the mountains, the trees and grass had grown back. We needed fresh water and from the screen I saw a huge lake. I told Rove to find a place and sit the ship down. I told him to stay cloaked. There were no sign of life, and I hoped it would be safe. Two hours later, we lifted off back to the darkness of space with our tanks full.

I retired to my room and took a quick shower then changed into my sleep clothes. Somewhere in my thoughts, I fell into a deep, peaceful sleep. I was not sure how long I had been asleep when I was awoken to someone calling my name. I lifted my head, looking around, and saw no one. It was the same voice as before. Who was this woman calling my name? I do not know why she was calling to me. I sat up to the side of the bed and gazed out the portal window. My heart beat with excitement—I was looking at a new cluster of stars. It was like a vision; no more than a dream. I knew we were in the galaxy of the Milky Way; I knew in my thoughts this is what I left my home of Ticoru for so long ago—what seemed like a lifetime. I left my home a young boy of twenty and was soon to be twenty-two. Look what has happened to me; look where I have been; the things I have seen. Looking through the portal, it made the trip worthwhile.

I called to the bridge and told the pilot to come to a full stop. "Wait for me, I am on my way." Of course, I told them to stay in stealth mode. I dressed quietly and ran to the bridge. I could not believe the beauty of the galaxy—looking through the screen it was breath taking. It was like nothing I had ever seen.

I said to my crew, "This is what we left home for; we have arrived in the Milky Way. Rove, find a planet where we can land." Working with the others, it did not take long to find what we were looking for. Meissa was the first small planet we charted. There was not much there, but we did manage to take on a few of the things we needed. The governor told me there were several planets in the system.

Our next stop was Betelgeuse—this was more of what I was looking for. The planet was very modern, with everything you could ask for. My crew wanted to come ashore. The governor asked us to stay if we wanted, and that is what we did. One week, we were back in space headed to Rigel. Rigel would be our last stop before we reached Earth. Jabel and I met with the governor. It was a great visit; more than anything, it was great to meet beings from other parts of the galaxy. Sitting in the chambers of the council and looking into the darkness of space, the view of the nebula was breath taking.

Looking through the big window was a bright and shining star I had to inquire about. The governor told me it was called Earth. In my mind, I thought this is where Zin and Cavota told me to go. I felt excited; I had accomplished a great task—the great task my father had bestowed on me. The governor and I talked for several hours until a sentry came to the governor.

The sentry said, "Governor, a ship has as to land; the captain is called Kalean." My heart went to my knees.

The governor said, "Paxton, you look weak." I tried to give him a hard copy of the events with Kalean.

He replied, "Paxton, there will be no trouble here from this Kalean." I only nodded my head. I thought, this was what the female voice on the ship told me—trouble follows. If this was it, so be it.

Kalean landed, not seeing my ship until he was on the ramp. I was standing beside the governor. Kalean froze when he saw me.

Kalean said, "Well, well, I have been looking for you. It appears you are invisible in your travels."

I smiled saying, "No Kalean, just my ship."

Kalean asked, "You are the governor here?" Replying, the governor said, "I am."

Kalean said, "I demand you take this man into custody."

The governor said, "Captain, you are in no position to make demands. This is my home; my planet. If you have a question about him, take it up with the planet council. While you are here you will respect me my world, my people, my laws, and my guest."

Kalean said, "If I do not?" The governor said, "Then it will be you in custody." Kalean started to back up, "Young one, I will see you in space." Kalean started up the ramp when another ship sat down two pads over. The hatch opened and the ramp went down. Walking down the ramp was a different kind of being; I did not know what to expect. Kalean watched this being approach him. I thought this must be one of Kalean's friends. He looked powerful; I wondered who he was. This being walked to the governor with his hand stretched out. "Greetings, governor." Bowing to him the governor said, "Greetings, sir. I was not expecting you." Whoever it was asked the governor about me.

Replying he said, "This is Paxton, captain of the ship Yon," pointing to my ship. This being is called Kalean, captain of this ship and a burden to young Paxton."

The being said while looking at me: "I am Toko, king of the Orion belt. I am here on a mission of King Zin." Kalean's head snapped and turned to look at me. "King Zin has informed me you were in this quadrant. I could have sent a sentry to watch, however I wanted to get away for a while. I told Zin I would take care of this myself." Looking at Kalean, Toko said, "Kalean, you will board your ship, leave Rigel, and never to return. If you are caught here again, you will be destroyed. It will be entered into the ship's log. You also will be escorted to the outer rim."

Kalean said as he boarded his ship, "I will see you in space." Kalean left into the darkness of space.

Governor Avi, Toko, and I had a lengthy conversation. Toko told me about the girl Shila, how she helped place him in power on Van Werth. Avi told me to stay the night if I wished. Toko stood then bid us farewell as he said he had to leave. Toko said, "I have done as my king has requested of me."

Toko said, "Paxton, beware of this Kalean; he will watch for your departure. You did say you were bound for Earth. Go in peace." Toko boarded his ship and left for the darkness of space. I told Avi I would leave early and then told Rove to secure the ship.

CHAPTER 8

THREE DAYS INTO FLIGHT FROM RIGEL, THE SHIP moved on. There were no sights of Kalean. One thing I could say was the Milky Way was a vast galaxy—thousands and thousands of stars and planets. We were deep inside Earth's galaxy when Rove called to me: "Captain, come to the bridge, please." Looking around, I moved closer. I said, "Rove, I am here."

Rove said, "Captain, there is a ship three light-years; they have not detected us. It is Kalean." Looking at the scope and then to the screen, I told Rove to come to a stop and stay cloaked. In seconds, Kalean's ship zipped us. He was so close, I thought he had hit us. I screamed, "Stay cloaked, Rove! Stay cloaked!" In seconds, the ship was gone. I walked to the star charts and called to Jabel. "Come over here." I saw a planet on the chart I wanted to check out; I surely did not want another fight with Kalean. I wanted to avoid all contact with anyone if possible. I gave Rove the coordinates. I wanted to bypass Kalean and this should do it—from our present location we were three hours away.

I am not afraid of Kalean, yet I want no fight that would place my crew in danger. There were two planets I wanted to see—this maybe would give Kalean the time to give up hunting me. I wanted to see Kepler and Promina. I was not sure if there were life or if it could sustain life on either; most of all, I was not sure we would be welcome if there were life.

It is possible these planets of the outer rim were the same as the Star of Joni. The two planets were not on the charts, yet there were small thin lines to and from—that only meant someone might have traveled there at their own risk.

I told Rove I was going to the galley. He sent me a jester of the hand. Walking down the corridor, I was thinking only of the planets when I heard the voice again: "Paxton, beware trouble ahead." "This is getting old," I said, "Who is there? Why can't you show yourself?" Nothing more was said. Walking on toward the galley, suddenly the ship went sideways. Yes, I do mean sideways—I thought we had been hit. I forgot about the galley, running to the bridge and holding on to whatever I could. The ship started to dive; I was falling to the floor just as a metal box flew by me. If the box had hit me, it surely have ended me.

The ship did level off which gave me the time to reach the bridge. I shouted to Rove, "What is happening?" as I entered the bridge.

Rove answered, "Captain, it is a turbulence storm as I have never seen." I looked at the scope then to the screen; I could see we were out of control—how my ship stayed together was beyond me. My ship was being tossed around like a leaf on the wind.

We were spinning so fast—as big as the ship was, it made no difference. From nowhere, something unbelievable happened: Rove gained control as if nothing ever happened. My thoughts went to the voice—danger ahead. Rove brought the ship to a full stop. Rove laid his head across his arms, leaning on the console.

Standing behind the captain's chair, I held tightly to the rail. I could see all were fine as I looked around. I called for a damage report; I was sure we had sustained quite a lot. How were we going to repair the ship here in space if there was damage? The ship was making strange sounds; the engineer said it was the way for the ship to say it was fine.

I looked at her, "I am not sure of that; walk with me, let us have a look around." Leaving the bridge, Mora and I walked the entire ship; it took more than two hours. We found no damage to say we could not continue. I told Rove to carry on; listen to the engines. I was fully aware that something was out there. I watched the screen as the planet came closer. The planet seemed as any other—just a ball in space. We were still a way out.

Rove flew the ship into the planet's atmosphere. The ship started to shake as we came closer. Flying closer, I could see there was a vast mountain range; there was snow on the peaks. My thought went to home, a place I wish to be now. As the ship flew at impulse speed, I knew I would never be the child I was when I left my home world. I had grown to be a fine captain—or at least I thought I had, with the crews help and the beings and friends I have made. I had become the adult my parents would be proud of. Rove calling to me brought me from where I was; he asked what my wish was. I told him to fly with the mountain range. Mora was watching the screen.

Mora said, "There is no sign of life or a building of any kind, captain—at least I see nothing." Rove took the ship up over two high peaks. From nowhere, two small ships appeared.

A voice called, "Identify yourselves."

Replying, I said, "I am Captain Paxton of the Ticoru vessel. We mean you no harm or disrespect. We were curious of the planet; we are travelers bound for the blue planet." I looked at Mora, "No life or ships."

Mora said, "Sorry captain, I did not see a thing or anyone. I still see no city."

The ship called again, "Follow me." After what seemed to be several miles, the small ship disappeared. It appeared to be a portal or a shield. We were going so fast, we could not stop or turn. Rove called, "Captain." I told him to go follow that ship. Passing through whatever it was we flew into, there was a city—a grand city. Now let me say, on Ticoru we had a beautiful city, but nothing as this.

A voice called, "Sit your ship down and wait for your escort." Rove did as instructed. Opening the hatch, we walked down the ramp. There were several beings at the bottom that appeared to be human. All were smiling as we approached with their hand outstretched, "Welcome! Welcome to Kepler. How did you find us? We are not known to the outsiders, as we call them." I tried to explain; I told him I had several questions to ask. He said the same. I told him about Kalean.

The man asked, "Is this being following you?" I told him I was not sure, as we were hiding in stealth the last time we met him. I want no trouble with him; I just want to go to Earth and see what it has to offer, then go back to my world.

The man said, "Come with us; tell your crew they may leave the ship. You need not fear, no one will board the vessel—this I assure you." I told Mora to come with me. Rove told the crew they may leave the ship but to return before night fall. Boarding the small craft, I must say the ride was short yet pleasing—it was a beautiful city.

I asked the one that seemed to be in charge about the turbulence we encountered. Smiling, he replied, "Just a precautionary defense; you will not encounter it when you depart. We like to call it our first line of defense."

I said, "If my ship was not in first class condition, it would have been torn apart." I asked the man his name—he told me he was called Berra. Berra said, "As we traveled, there were ships moving around that we wish not to meet." He also told me he was the governor of Kepler.

The tram started to slow down as we approached a marvelous building—it was as grand as grand could be; more like a palace.

I spoke out loud, saying: "Not even the palace of Boldlygo was like this."

Berra said, "Boldlygo—you have seen this place?" I told him I was there once. Berra told me he had never left the planet of Kepler; he had been here his whole life. "I have heard of this place. Our King Toko of Van Werth has told us of Boldlygo. He said King Zin helped place him into power. Toko is a fair being, this I can say. He knows how to take care of his people, beings, and humans."

"Berra," I said, "I met Toko on Rigel. Toko delivered to me a message from Zin. Zin is the same; he loves his people as well as the other beings on the planet. Zin has alliance with several planets throughout the universe—including the Orion."

Berra nodded, "Yes, that is what I have been told. Come, my friend; let's go inside."

Several delegates waited at a huge table as we approached—they knew I was coming. Each member stretched out their hand and gave me a greeting, which I returned. I introduced Mora. One asked, "Is she your mate?" I told them she was my engineer officer.

The main one said, "We understand you are on your way to the blue planet called Earth." I told them I would have been there if the ship following me was not trying to destroy me.

Berra said, "Yes, why is that, young one? You never said."

"I tell you I have never met this being until he tried to blow me and my crew out of space. If not for Cavota and the people of the Moon of Spores, we would be dead. I suppose he wants power. The ship suffered heavy damage to the main hull and to the life support. Cavota helped me and this is when I went to Boldlygo."

One said, "So this planet is real?"

Smiling I said, "Oh, it is very real. I might add they have unicorns—I have seen them with my own eyes. Several thousand years ago, their leader placed them in a hidden valley until the time was right for them to live with man again. Boldlygo is a paradise in space. I assure you their king is a just man. He loves his people." Berra and I talked while the others looked on, with a question now and then of different things. I did not tell them anything that would give them too much about the planet; I should not have told them of the unicorns.

I stood from the table and told Berra it was getting late. "I need to return to my ship. Mora and I would like to return to check on my crew. I truly would like to reach Earth in the next few months, if possible." Each delegate said as they took my hand that it was a pleasure to me us; I told them the same. Berra told me as I stepped from the tram that beyond the turbulence, I would be on my own. He also told me to forget about Promina. "Paxton, there is no life there; only terrible things." Well, I took him at his word—I did not go; Rove had the engines running at idle. Securing the ramp and the hatch, Rove lifted the ship up to the darkness of space.

Mornings come and evenings go—the only thing about space is it is always dark. I changed from my sleeping attire to my captain's suit. Walking to the galley for tea, I also wanted something to eat. My meal was great, made from a small bowl of fruit. I was standing near the window portal when Rove called for me to come to the bridge. Rove reported that there was no activity to report. "Captain," he said, "it was a good night." I relieved Rove from the chair. I took the seat as we continued to press on. I looked at the screen as Mora said "Oh no." I stood, looking excited, and asked Mora: "Are we cloaked?"

Mora replied, "Yes, captain; and sir—it is a ship. It appears to be the same, captain. It is Kalean." I thought this being just want give up. I said, "Bring the ship to full stop."

Mora said, "Captain, you have the control."

"I suppose I do, Mora," I spoke. "I am not used to that."
Kalean's ship came to a complete stop. There was complete
silence on board. For a split moment, he circled above us
they went to hyper-space. My thoughts were we will be safe
for a while. I watched the screen for several minutes—were
we lucky or was he really gone?

The ship flew on through space without another encounter from Kalean. Looking at the screen and through
the portal window, I thought nothing could be this good—
he was out there somewhere.

Mora told me the planet of Saturn was coming up in
the next few minutes. I could not believe the beauty of the
planet—looking at the charts, there never has been life here.
I thought it was a shame; I wanted to see the planet closer.
The charts did say it was not recommended. The charts said
to make our turn to line up with Mars. On the screen appeared a small blimp—it was Kalean.

What drives a being to want this much power? Is it that
important to have the power to destroy? Kalean is on a
power trip; someone somewhere will end that for him. Until
then, he will destroy anything to show that he is the master
of power. I have never seen such a being as him. Kalean's
ship disappeared as it appeared; he went to hyperspace
somewhere in the vast darkness of space.

Kalean's ship was a fully contained battleship; it was massive. I often wondered where his home world was. Did his
people build this ship? Were there other ship as this? Most of

all—were all his people like him? I suppose it did not matter; the size of the ship could destroy a small planet. Zin should have destroyed Kalean. Maybe he should have let one of the girls do it; maybe Zin was waiting on me to do that.

My ship was powerful, there was no doubt about that. Cavota made sure of that by placing powerful weapons on board, plus the cloaking device. If I caught him off guard, I might take him out; maybe even take out his life support. Even as I thought this, I knew I could—not without help. Here in the darkness of space, where would I find help?

Rove approached the planet of Mars. Dropping to the altitude of the planet, I noticed it was a very desolate place, nothing but dirt as far as one could see. The atmosphere was not breathable, so we had to stay on the ship. Looking on the screen, I wondered why it was even here. Rove sat the ship down along a ridge that seemed to go forever; I thought was this planet eve habitual. Did someone live here maybe thousands of years ago? I suppose it will remain a mystery.

The crew and I spent three days on the floor of this forsaken planet, staying in stealth; hiding from Kalean. We were learning and watching. On more than one occasion, violet storms erupted. Stones and dirt were moving at a tremendous speed. From the inside of the bridge, we could hear the debris hitting the hull of the ship. I had no fear; the ship could resist it. Rove took the ship back up above the storm as he had on several occasions. Watching through the scope, I began to understand why nothing could live here. Gazing into the darkness of space, I heard a small whisper in my ear. Turning, I saw no one. The voice said, "Stay here." The crew was at their duties, so who was talking to me? Who was making this whisper? Before we reached the Moon of Spores was the first time. It was a female, but who? Who was she, and where did she come from? Was this a ghost ship? I did not believe in that, not for a moment. I do believe that someday I will find out who she is and why she comes to me.

Leaving Rove with the ship, I went to the galley for a small meal. I was hungry since I had not had a meal in a while. Entering the galley, I had a cup of tea and my meal. Walking to my table, I sipped my tea while gazing through the window. Looking upon the planet, it seemed so small from our position in space. I knew we were safe if we stayed here and remained cloaked. The time will come when we must leave—then it would be on and a fight I did not want. The one thing I could say about Kalean was he was ambitious; he meant to destroy and kill everyone on board.

From well beyond the Moon of Spores to our present location, I knew Kalean was out there somewhere. I also knew he meant to take me down. I could understand this if somewhere in our past I had wronged him.

Kalean knew we were going to Earth. He also knew we would need to come this way. Going off the path had occurred to me, yet I knew what that meant—it meant traveling uncharted space. I feel in the earth's atmosphere is where he will make his move. Sitting here in the view of the planet of Mars, knowing Earth was the next planet, I would tell the crew to always be alert.

Returning to my room from the galley, I took a bath, changed into my sleeping clothes, and checked the star charts. Looking at Earth, it was a big ball sitting in space—I got a thrill to know I would be the first of my family to travel this far out into space.

I stretched out on the bed and started to have thoughts; this sometimes bothered me, for the fact were that I could not go to sleep. I sure needed sleep; I was exhausted. Thinking of my parents, I wondered if they ever thought of me; did they wonder if I was alive or dead? I would like to think they thought of me often. Turning to my side, somewhere in the night I fell asleep.

I was not sure how long I had been asleep when suddenly my eyes opened. Someone was calling to me. Looking around my room, I saw no one. "Paxton," the voice called; it was the same female. I sat to the side of the bed and gazed into an empty room.

I ask, "Why can I not see you?"

"Paxton, do not fear me, for I am here in sprit. King Zin has asked me to check on you from time to time. We have never met, yet I know who you are. Zin asked in my meditation to watch over you. Paxton, you will soon reach Earth. It will be hard for you. No more can I say except that your life will change—just remember to try to adjust. Always keep an open mind; there will be new people that will come into your life. Stay here above this desolate planet and do not venture forward yet. Wait, watch, and you will know when the time is right. Changes will come; you will not understand at first but Paxton, all has been seen."

There was silence for a moment. The moment was so quiet, it was eerie. A shiver ran over me; looking around I was alone.

"Are you still here?" I asked. Looking around again, there was only me and the coolness of the room. I stood and walked to the portal. For some reason, my thoughts went home to Ticoru, my home to the beautiful ice capped mountains with the luscious fertile valley below. I thought of my mother and father. How long had it been? I was twenty-one when I left, soon to be twenty-four. Look where I have gone—I have ventured into several galaxies and planets. I suppose you could say I was a great explorer.

I thought of all the beauty I left behind in my world; I thought of my people—the mountains, the stream, the cool breeze on my face. Then a smile come to my face as it did when Leah told me of the unicorn. I thought if we had them on Ticoru, what a world it would be. I will write in the captains log of all the places I have seen, all the places I have been, and the planet of Boldlygo is the one place I will never forget. I can tell people I have seen a unicorn; they won't believe me. Do they exist on other worlds?

Changing into my uniform, I went to the galley for tea. Several crew members were there having an enjoyable time;

it was great their spirits were so high. One did ask how long
we were to stay. I took my tea and smiled, then said, "Until
we leave." That was all I said. Rove said good morning as
I passed him; I returned the jester. Rove joined me on the
walk to the bridge. "Captain, nothing to report. All is good;
the only thing moving is the storm on the planet floor."

I relived Rove and took my chair. I thought as I looked
at the screen about the voice that called to me in the night.
Why did this person come to me? How does she know me—
yet, who is she? Could it be my imagination playing tricks
on my mind, or was she real? Sipping my tea, I decided she
was real. Like she said, she was in sprit; there was no other
way to look at it.

Sitting here in space, time seems to drag. I knew it was
not time to leave; I knew Rove would be here soon for his
shift. I walked to the chart table as Rove entered the bridge.
We talked for a while as I informed him of the events. I told
him everything was great.

Rove asked, "Captain, how much longer are we to stay
here?" I told him until the time is right for us to leave. Rove
took the chair as I turned to leave. Rove asked, "Captain,
you are leaving?" I told him we would continue our talk
later; I told him to have the crew check everything. "I want
the ship in top shape when we leave. The way I see it, two
months to Earth; maybe three. There will be nowhere to
hide if we are attacked. Rove, the only thing that bothers me
is where Kalean is." I walked away from the bridge.

CHAPTER 9

IT WAS GOOD TO BE BACK TO SCHOOL. SOPHIA AND I had not indulged in a lengthy conversation since we had returned from Tasha's. I must say, it was a different kind of vacation; it will be one I will never forget. Sophia would do what she had to do, as would I. Sometimes, she would pass my room and stop—never saying a word, just staring at me. I was getting tired of this bullshit; I could zap her as I did the closet door. Then I thought, what would she do to me? I knew she had powers of some kind; the only thing was that I didn't know what were they, and how strong Sophia was. I really did not want to find out. I only wanted my life back the way it was before. For some reason, I do not think that will ever happen again. I believe in so many ways, my life was going to change and it would take me to places I have only dreamed of.

Time comes and goes; school was the same, as always—Nina was always lurking around, trying to see and hear conversation. I do not like her; I never have. I do believe if she gets the chance, she would kill me. I know something she did not know—I will send her packing if she tries anything. School was coming to winter break soon; snow had fallen the night before.

Sometimes, I would have a dream of sun filled days lying on a beach somewhere. In my life, I had only seen the ocean once. I was six or seven. I really could not say why I was there or where I was going. Truthfully, the ocean did not amaze me. I prefer dirt and grass with trees and the mountains, like the ones at the border of Russia and Ukraine.

In my thoughts, my mind went to Nina. I could tell she wanted to hurt me. I always could, since the first time we met when she was near, like now. I was sitting on my bed when the bitch appeared at the door. She just stood gazing at me through her piercing dark eyes. Nina was pure evil, I could feel it. Nina took two steps closer to me, then stopped. I was getting ready to smack her ass.

Nina said, "Good morning, Mimi. How are you today?"

I asked, "Nina, do you really care? I mean you never have, so why now?"

Nina said, "That is no way to be. I am sorry about the first part of the year, Mimi."

I said, "Nina, you have never liked me since I have been here; you seem to be jealous of me and Sophia. Just to let you know, Sophia and I are cousins or something—I was told this by Sophia's aunt, Tasha."

Nina said, "Yes Mimi—or something." I made a face as she left the room to mock her. Nina left my room as I stood from my bed. I walked to the door and watched her as she walked down the hallway to the stairs. I closed my eyes and pushed out just enough to make her stumble; I snickered. Sophia came from nowhere and said, "Excellent job, Mimi." Well, hell—I did not know what to think.

Sophia called the class to order. I watched each girl come into the room. Nina was not among them—this made me believe she might be a little frightened. Then it occurred to me: Nina was not afraid of me or anything; I mean, how could she believe I made her stumble? Sophia taught the class for two hours then told us to enjoy the rest of the day.

Walking up the stairs, I went to my room, put on my boots and a heavy coat because it was cold outside with the fresh snow that fell the night before. I opened the door, looked down the hallway, and there was no one around. I went outside down the steps. I had a special place I like to go to—it was oven a small ridge by a huge old rock. It was a cropping of rocks that looked as if someone placed them there hundreds of years ago. I found it one day while I was out walking; this was shortly after I arrived here at the school. Now I love to go there when I was bored, as I was then . I really could lose myself in thought when I came here.

I walked to the huge rock, looking into the sky only to see the snow fall. Winter had come to Russia and the village of Vologda. The village did not have much to offer; it was a small farm village. In the summer, when the vegetables were harvested, everyone got together. You would think as the modern times with all the technology that spaceships would be everywhere. Did I say that? Walking on, I went to my favorite place by the rock. I slung my pack to the ground, took out my blanket and my book, and started to read.

I started reading of a family from long ago. The woman in question was Lola, whoever she was. I suppose an hour had passed; I stopped and stretched out on the blanket. Looking upward, nighttime was coming. I had been here two hours—how this day flew by!

I found myself in a strange place. I remember closing my eyes for a moment. I had drifted into the past; a place hundreds of years ago. Wait—I was there, in life. I was living this, yet it was in my thoughts. Whatever it was, I was enjoying it. I opened my eyes; damn, it is daylight—surely I did not sleep through the night. I thought, have I been here all night? Wait it was dark, now it is light—what the hell is going on here?

I opened the book again. I read how this woman Lola met this man Comp. Wait, this made little sense; where this was going? There was someone named Ject, Ira, and two children in tubes. What the hell was happening? I heard this sound, as if something was in the forest. I jumped up and packed my things. Looking around, I saw nothing. Taking in a big breath of fresh air with my head tilted back, I looked into the heavens above. Trust me, I had no idea what I was looking at. I mean, I had only heard of them; only seen them in pictures. There was no mistaking it—it was a UFO. It was hovering no more than fifteen-hundred feet above me. Russian planes were all over it, then it just zipped through the air damn fast—I assure you, there was nothing that fast in the Russian air force. I slung my pack on my back and ran as fast as I could; I thought they were watching me.

I ran as fast as I could over the small ridge through the forest across the school grounds. I ran through the door; I was as white as the clouds on a summer day. I ran right into Sophia. She looked at me with those crystal eyes. Sophia asked, "You want to talk about it?"

"Talk about what?" I said.

Sophia said, "Do not play with me, little girl. I will kick your ass." "Really, Sophia? We have been back for almost a month with hardly a word, then all you can say is you will kick my ass?! Bring it on." Well, I should not have said that.

Sophia said, "Not on your best day, Mimi, do you want to try that." I laughed out loud; so did Sophia. I asked Sophia if she had seen Nina. She told me she was staying in her room—well, that was fine by me. Sophia did ask where I had been since I was late coming in. I told her about my evening and what I had seen in the forest. She told me she had seen the same thing from the terrace. I asked, "What do you think it was?" She said, "It was a ship of some sort; you know, a UFO."

Sophia and I talked long into the night. I told her about my reading in my book of the woman named Lola. Sophia smiled and said that was a long time ago, Mimi.

Sophia said she was going home next week. "It will begin the winter break. There will be no one here. Would you like to come with me? I will be gone the rest of the year; I am sure Tasha would love to see you and talk to you. It will be easier now since you know some of the history. Mimi, by the way, I am not your cousin—I am your aunt, your father's sister. Your father was one of the very few men born to the earth family. Believe me Mimi, he was strong with this power thing."

I asked, "Then where did—or how did—you get powers?" Sophia laughed loud and said, "I do not have powers, Mimi; hell, I am just a mean woman." Well, now she had to make me believe that.

"Mimi, Tasha will die soon. If you come with me, you can ask her whatever you wish. She will answer anything you ask. The only thing I can tell you is it is real—I am sure you have read it before. Someday, someone will come."

I looked at Sophia and said to her: "Sophia, I think they're already here." I started to my room, then Sophia said to me, "Mimi, I love you. Have a good night and sleep well." I cannot remember anyone telling me they love me in so many years. I went to my room, took a bath, put on my pj's, then laid across my bed. Closing my eyes, I drifted to a more pleasant place.

Someone called to me. Opening my eyes, I found myself in a simpler place and time; a different time of long ago. I was walking about what seemed to be a farm. There were farm animals—cows, sheep, and horses. I was dreaming, there were no doubt. Something touched my hand and that brought me wide awake. A girl was standing beside my bed.

"Mimi, please do not be afraid," she said. I told her I was not afraid of a dream. "Oh Mimi, is it just a dream to you? My dear, you are the last living member of our Earth family." The girl was dressed in a very strange attire. She reached out to me to take my hand. "Come with me, Mimi." I walked beside her for a while.

I asked, "What is your name?" "Oh Mimi," she said, "names are not important. Yet I suppose that is who we are. I am the one person you would never expect to see here. You dream of me; talk to me—yet you do not know me."

"Oh my, you are Hannah. I have had dreams of you since I was a small child." "Mimi, you called to me many years ago; I was only twelve. Then you called again when I was fifteen. I have come to you and watched over you the best I could. Well, with the help of Sophia—Sophia took you to Tasha. Tasha is incredibly old to be on Earth. Tasha would never tell how old she is, but she is so intelligent. My mother come to Tasha once; my mother brought Mayrra back to our world. You must tell Tasha that Mayrra is wonderful. She has a child; Mayrra is the Queen of the Claxton tribe."

I said, "Damn I am glad this shit is a dream; I almost believed what you were saying." Hannah took my hand and bent my fingers back. "Does that feel like a dream, Mimi?" I woke up screaming. Sophia was the first to reach me.

Sophia placed her arms under me, bringing me to her chest. "Mimi, what is wrong?" I was trembling with fright. My finger hurt so bad. Looking at my index finger, it was blue and swollen. My tears would not stop flowing down my cheeks. Sophia closed the door to the hallway and told the girls to go back to bed. "I will stay here with Mimi for a while; I will try to calm her down."

Sitting on the side of the bed, Sophia asked me what had happened. I tried to tell her, I really did. My finger was hurting so bad; words would not come. Sophia took my hand, "Mimi, how, or what, did you do?" I told her about the dream.

Sophia said, "You know Mimi, I have heard of out of body experiences before. Shila was the best, her and Fina— they could go anywhere. That is how they found the others here. Who in your dream did this to you?" I told her the one I have dreamed of since I was a little girl. "It was Hannah!"

Sophia said, "I do remember you telling me of her. In fact, you talked about her on numerous occasions." I sat in silence for a moment. "Sophia, Hannah's mother is the one that took Mayrra back to their would. Wherever that is,

Sophia." Sophia placed a small bag of ice on my hand; the pain did not stop but is did stop the throbbing.

I turned to let my feet and legs hang from the bed. I was still crying, wondering what the hell was going on. I leaned my head to Sophia's shoulder. "Sophia" I said, "please tell me what is happing to me and why is this happening now?"

Replying Sophia said, "Mimi, we tried to tell you of this when we were at Tasha's, but you wanted no part of it." "Well, I do now. Please tell me everything." Sophia told me when she was a small child, she had been taught that someday someone would come. "That only means that someday, if you live long enough, you will see something wonderful. Tasha told me that on a planet called Boldlygo, when a female comes of age she gets power." "Sophia we're on Earth, not this planet you spoke of." She said when a female leaves Earth, the closer they come to the planet, the stronger they would become. I can only repeat what I hear or have been taught.

"Mimi, come home with me; let us talk to Tasha. I promise you will not be disappointed. We can learn together; we can call to Hannah and she will come. It appears she is strong with power, like her mother."

My finger hurt badly, yet the pain was going away. The only thing I knew was Hannah was a bitch for doing this— had that been Nina, I would have kicked her ass. I do know it was real.

Sophia left for her room. I laid back in my bed, covered up, and drifted off to sleep. Something moving on the bed woke me—it was Hannah. "Did you come to finish me this time? This is bullshit," I said as much.

Hannah laughed out loud. "You humans and your language phrases." Hannah told me her mother says that all the time; her and Fina.

I asked, "Hannah, what is it you want with me? You have taunted me in my dreams since I was a small child."

Hannah said, "I do not want anything from you, Mimi. You called to me."

I asked, "How did I call to you Hannah, when I never knew you? The only thing I can remember is one morning I woke up and whispered your name. Now, after all this time you come to me; that is what I am asking."

Hannah said, "When you called, I was with King Zin of Boldlygo. I told Zin about you. Zin said he thought Mayrra was the last and we wondered if there are others. Zin asked me to come to you if you called again. You see, Mimi, sometimes when a person dreams, they do not really know what they do. Calling to someone is a way for your conscious mind to deal with your subconscious. I like to keep it simple by saying it is reality. Mimi, you now are dreaming."

"Bullshit," I said, "tell that to my finger, bitch." Hannah laughed out loud. "Leah started that word long ago when Dorn brought her to Boldlygo."

I ask, "Are you from Boldlygo, Hannah?" Hannah told me she was not. She said she was from a planet called Galaxo. "Humans settled their hundreds of years ago; there is a species called Claxton's. Fina is half Claxton; my husband is half Claxton." I asked Hannah what part she plays on her world. She smiled and said, "Mimi, I am the queen; my husband Jawah is king." I said, "Bullshit." We laughed at the saying. "Mimi, I must go, but you must go home with Sophia. My mother wants to see Tasha—they do know one another. My mother wants to talk to Sophia. Go with Sophia, and we will come to you at the house of Tasha when the time is right. I must go now." Hannah took my hand, and the swelling and pain left. I went to sleep—it was the best sleep I have ever had in my life.

A movement outside my door brought me wide awake. I looked from my bed to the window; I could see the gray steal of the morning; this told me it was almost time to rise. Sophia would be making her rounds soon. I walked slowly to the door and easily turned the doorknob to peep outside. Nina smiled at me, smiling like a small child with a basket of candy.

Nina said, "You little bitch, who do you think you are? Sophia treats you as if you are her child. Well, Mimi, I am going to kick your ass, here and now." Well, that is all it took for me. I raised my hand, feeling the power inside of me; power I have never witnessed before. My hands flew up and Nina went down. She was choking and gasping for air.

I said, "What was it you said Nina? You called me a bitch. Believe me Nina, you are the bitch." I had her on the floor; I wanted to kick her in the face. My leg came up and I was going to Bruce Lee her ass. I was furious at her; my long dark hair was flying around my head. I wanted to hurt this girl—I wanted to kill her. I believe I would have done just that, I was that pissed off at her. I started to follow through when two girls yelled at me. Sophia came up behind me. She had this look, like let someone try to stop me; it would have been an awfully terrible thing.

Sophia said, "What is going on here? Someone speak."

I replied, "She called me a bitch. Mimi said she was going to kick my ass here and now. I suppose she fell."

Sophia said, "Really, Mimi?"

I said, "Yes Sophia, ask her?" All Nina could do was shake her head. I smiled as I closed my door—Sophia never said another word.

Time comes and goes. Two days after the incident, Nina had yet to show for class. Each day Sophia asked about her—if something was wrong with her, no one was saying so.

Sophia dismissed the class, telling us to go outside. I remained in my seat until the other girls left the room. Walking to the door, I could see they had gathered in a half circle at the bottom of the steps.

I walked back to my room and took my heavy coat from the closet. I was planning to go to my special place among the rocks. Leaving the school, I could see Sophia walking up the stairs; I knew where she was going.

I placed my coat around me as I walked to the door. Winter had come once more to the small town of Vologda, Russia. There was not very much to see here in Vologda— our small village was only a small farm village. I stood on the stoop watching the girls throw snowballs. I was not sure what the girls would do; I did not care. Since leaving Tasha's before, I was Mimi—from that day until now, I knew no one would ever hurt me again.

I walked down the steps to the yard. The girls moved apart. I stopped in the middle of them. I was getting all choked up, like most girls did when they felt alone. I said to them, "I am not a freak." One of the girls said, "Then what are you? Nina is my friend. Because of you she is afraid to leave her room."

I said, "Nina has picked on me and bullied me since the day I arrived here at school. I have tried to be friends with her—every one of you here have done the same. I will say this only once: leave me the hell alone or I will hurt you. I do not wish to be like this." I walked on through the crowd to the edge of the yard.

Nina had parents, so I was not sure why she was here. The girls that were here come from around the village and towns.

Walking through the soft, fallen snow, I found my special place. I dropped my pack to the ground. I took my heavy wrap from my pack, wrapping it around me. I looked around; I saw no one. I took my small book in hand and settled down and started to read. My thoughts stopped me; this I will ask Sophia about. I stood and pushed the snow with my foot. The wind blew hard as to say I was not supposed to do that. Snow started to blow around me like a whirlwind; I was completely covered with snow. My mind seemed to go blank; my world as I knew it was gone. I was drifting somewhere, traveling a million miles an hour. Where was I going? What was happing to me? I cried for Sophia, "Help me, Sophia!"

Opening my eyes to a new horizon, I found myself in a place I did not know. Where am I? It was a vast open place. I could never live in a place as this. Behind me a voice spoke, "Well, that is too bad for you Mimi; I was going to ask to come here."

"Who are you?" I asked.

Replying she said, "I am Shila, mother of Hannah. Hannah said she came to you." "Hannah never said I was to come live here," I said. Shila stood looking at me.

I asked, "Why are you staring at me?" Shila told me I had quite the look. She said like maybe DNA of Leah and Adair. "I do not know who that is," I said. Shila told me we were the descendants of Lola and Comp. "Many generations have passed; we thought Mayrra was the last. We knew of Sophia. Yes, she is family—not real blood as you and Tasha. My king has come to Tasha many times, this is how she knows so much about us. Mimi, all females born with the DNA gene have powers. Some are strong, like me and Leah. The list goes on."

I asked, "Shila, why did you bring me here?"

Shila said, "Mimi, I live on Galaxo, where you are in spirit—a dream as to say and yes, a real dream—without the broken finger. My king asked me to come to you." Another voice spoke, "I too, am here, Shila." I turned to see a beautiful woman, so pure I fell to my knees; I thought she was an angel. She stretched out her hands, "Rise, Mimi."

She said, "I am Kayla, wife of Ira. We are here to talk to you of coming events. These events will take place over time; these events will cause certain things to happen in your world. Then Mimi, you will come home to us, if you wish." All at once, females come from a light. They called themselves the women of Boldlygo—from Queen Tressa, and the list went on.

From Galaxo, it was Hannah, Fina, and Mayrra, and each one was telling me of different events. Leah told me in space that a war was being fought between two ships; this would cause a disturbance on earth. "I assure you it will happen; Zin has seen this. You, Sophia, and Tasha will take part in these events. You must go home with Sophia."

I asked, "What is to happen when this is over, and why me?"

Kayla said, "Mimi, you can come here to Galaxo or to Boldlygo." I looked at Mayrra and asked "Where you live?"

Mayrra said, "I live here, Mimi; I love it here. I live in the city of the Claxtons. You cannot go there."

I asked, "Then why are you there?" Mayrra told me she was the queen; her mate was RA; he is king. "You could come here or stay on earth; there is a young man on the ship that will escape. You and Sophia will become friends. Mimi, we must go. Go home with Sophia."

A soft hand touched my shoulder through the snow. Opening my eyes and looking up, it was Sophia.

Sophia said, "Well, did you sleep well, young lady?" I never said a word. I stood and shook off the snow while looking around; the snow was six inches deeper than before. Sophia said, "Let's go back to the school." Still in a daze, I said, "Sophia, why are you here?"

Sophia said, "Mimi, you were calling to me, that is how I found you. You were shouting for me to help you." My eyes began to water as I followed Sophia through the snow. For the next two days, the school went on as usual. I asked Sophia why Nina was here. I said the girls here were mostly orphans, like me; some from broken homes. Sophia told me Nina was a very rebellious girl—her parents could do nothing with her. "I do not believe she will be back. I explained to them what had happened, and they agreed to place her somewhere else." I promise that did not bother me; I was glad to see the bitch go.

Sophia asked, "Well, young lady, did you have a good nap?" I never said a word. I stood looking at the snow that had piled up where I was laying. Sophia said, "Let's get back to the school, Mimi. It is going to be a long wintry night." Walking back to the school, I could not believe how much snow had fallen. I also did not know how long I had been asleep—the only thing I knew was the snow was deep and cold.

I asked Sophia as we walked, "Why were you here?" Sophia told me it was getting late and she was worried about me; she said she could hear me calling to her, that is how she found me. She said I was screaming for her to help. My eyes watered as I followed Sophia through the snow.

School was open for the next two days. On the second day, Sophia dismissed the class. She told the girls as they left to enjoy the time away. I found this the time to ask her about Nina.

I asked, "Sophia, why was Nina here at the school? The girls here are mostly like me—they are orphans or from broken homes." Nina was so rebellious; she had been expelled from every school around. Tasha knew her parents, so she took her in. She said her parents could not do anything with her. "Mimi, I do not believe she will be back. I explained what had happened to her parents; I believe they will send her to another place." I assure you, that did not make me mad—I was glad to see the bitch go.

Sophia asked if I was coming home with her. I told her I did not have a choice and that I would explain on the way. Leaving through the main door, I saw the caretaker in the front room. I had never seen him before; I said as much to Sophia. There was nothing else said of him.

Sophia drove on as I talked to her about the dream I was having when she found me in the forest.

Sophia said, "Well, Mimi, I was wondering who you were talking to." I also told her they asked me to come to their world to live. I told her of the person on the ship; I told her it was so real that I even know his name. Sophia told me to tell Tasha everything. "I am sure she will be pleased to hear about Mayrra. Do not leave anything out—what was said, tell her."

The ride took longer since the snow did not let up; the road was so piled up and slick. Several times, Sophia slid sideways and would say whoa, then laugh. Sophia said it usually took forty-five minutes, but today it took an hour and a half. I suppose in the time we have left the school, ten inches had fallen. The roads were getting treacherous. I was happy when we arrived at the house. Sophia told me to bring my night bag, and Ivan would bring the rest before morning. Reaching into the back, I took my bag as she asked.

Standing in the driveway, looking at the huge house with snow all around it, I thought about how beautiful it looked. Tasha was sitting in her big chair in front of that huge window; Tasha stretched out her hand.

Tasha said, "Mimi, it is so good to see you again. I hear you have had a meeting with someone." My eyes shifted to

Sophia. "How would you know that, Tasha?" I asked. Tasha told me she could see things others could not. I do believe her.

Sophia and I sat long into the night talking to Tasha. The last thing I told Tash about before going to my room was about Mayrra. I told Tasha Mayrra was a queen of a clan called the Claxtons and that Mayrra married a king. I can only say it was a dream, but she said to tell you she loved you very much." I walked to the window smiling and said good night to them.

CHAPTER 10

SOMEWHERE IN SPACE, WE WERE HIDING IN THE earth galaxy; hiding from the one thing that could destroy us—a means to an end, unless we could escape the wrath of Kalean. We sat several days as it is in space, since it was always dark. My only hope to reach Earth was that we do not have an encounter, yet I knew it was wishful thinking; I knew there would be no escape. The next time we meet, it will be to the death of him or me.

I left the galley for the bridge. Entering, Rove told me there was no sign of Kalean in the time we had been here. Mora said, "Captain, Kalean has appeared only once, then he went to hyperspace." I took my chair while looking at the screen; there was nothing but stars. I told Rove to come as close to the earth's moon as he could get.

Rove said, "Captain, this won't be a problem; it is what lays beyond the moon that will be the problem—that is where we will encounter Kalean." I knew he was right, but one can hope. Rove told me when we come from stealth somewhere between the moon and Earth, it will all come together.

I thought, if we are hit and the crew must abandon ship, at least my crew was all human. My crew could fit in on Earth if it came to that. Kalean's crew were not even close to human; they would be destroyed if they went to Earth. In second thought, maybe we could hide in an asteroid field—yet there were no such thing here; I have searched the charts.

Mora walked around the bridge. The crew members waited to play their game; some were watching the instruments. Standing, I walked to the huge screen.

I said, "Mora, message all the crew." Mora switched to the ship's intercom.

I said, "Could I please have your attention—this is your captain. We will be leaving the atmosphere of the planet Mars tomorrow; it is time to continue our journey to Earth; it is a month away. You know as I do Kalean is out there somewhere. When we leave here, we must always be on our guard. Since we left our home world, this being has tried to destroy us more than once. If your duty calls for you to be at the screen, do not look away for any period—always be focused; stay alert. Remember, Kalean wants to destroy us. I wish all the best, but if it comes to the point to abandon ship, do not hesitate. The pods are programed for Earth. Please take care; we will leave soon."

I thought hard about the message I delivered to my crew; it was a pleasure to serve with them. I surely did not want anything to happen to anyone. I thought I should turn and run—there is no shame in running. I have always said it is better to run and return to fight another day. I could not run; it was not in me. My crew, if any survive, will be fine if they reach the pods. If Kalean attacks me, I will do my best to destroy him. I will hope for the best, expect the worst.

Suddenly, my thoughts went home to Ticoru. Since the day we left, I have often wondered if we will ever see our home world. If I do, I hope we all make it; one could only hope. I made another announcement. I told the crew that tonight, we will go to the galley and have drinks. If this night were to be the last night, we could celebrate; I wanted it to be a good one. I told them not to worry; no one could detect us. As we are sitting still, we are not giving off heat or vapor. Tonight, we will be a family. I thought it would be our last time, but I kept this to myself.

The day ended as everyone made their way to the galley. The big screen set the mode. I had Rove to take the ship to the planet at about ten thousand feet. I admit it was a beautiful place, even with the violent storms. The galley master opened the bar at my request. I must say everyone was having a fun time—there was laughter and dancing; games were being played; some watched the storm dance across the planet floor. It was a desolate place, yet so beautiful—there were high mountains and desert everywhere. If somewhere in time a colony lived here, it had to be rough on them. Who knows what laid beneath the surface. What mystery was in a canyon was beyond me. I did write in my journal that I found no sign of ancient life. What did I know? I was a pilot, not a scientist. I was the captain and I loved it. If Kalean was out there— and I knew he was—I hoped he let me live long enough to let me see Earth and talk to some of the people there. I had no way of knowing what the future held.

I knew I would find out in the few weeks to come; I knew I would see things other will not; I would be on Earth. My crew mostly dead or scattered across Earth, like the rocks and dirt that is scattered on this planet floor.

I believe most knew what to expect—some knew they would never see home again. This crew was made up of good people, as solid as they come. I was their captain, and as their captain I was close to only a few. If Kalean attacks, I only hope all make it off the ship. If Kalean comes at me in space, that is one thing—if he comes at me in the earth's atmosphere, that could prove disaster not only for Earth, but their people. I could not allow this to happen. Life is short regardless; I have made my decision. If Kalean comes at me, I will try to evacuate as many as I can. I will then hit him head on or nosedive into Kalean's ship. I feel this would be the honorable thing to do; then if time allows, I will try to slip into an escape pod.

Several thousand feet above the planet floor of Mars, I stood in front of the big portal. We were close enough to witness the storm that swept across the planet. In my lifetime I have never seen such storms as here. I smiled as I watched the crew—I let them enjoy the night before I made my speech. This would be one of the last I would make. It seemed hours had passed when I went before them. Tapping on the glass, I got their attention. Each one turned to me with the look of concern. I could read some of their thoughts; it appeared they knew what I was going to say. This is something I did not do often because I did not need to—my crew knew me, after all we had been together for an exceedingly long time.

I said, "My crew, you know I am not good at this. First, let me say I could not be prouder of a crew as the one that stands before me. I know along the way, we have lost friends, made other friends, and had good times as well as bad. Believe me, I cannot say what tomorrow will bring; I cannot tell you what the coming days will be. The only thing I can say is it has been a pleasure to serve as your captain. I would and could fly with you forever." I pointed to the outside. "Kalean is out there somewhere. I cannot say what he has on his mind, or what he is going to do—the one thing I can say is he plans to destroy this ship. My friends, please. If I tell you to abandon ship, please do not hesitate—go as fast as you can to the escape pods. They are already programed for Earth. Each pod will hold six people. When you reach

Earth, you will be fine; you can blend in with the earth people. The most important thing is do not wait for me. Release the pods, and hopefully we will meet again. Leave your beacon on; maybe someone will find you."

I turned to leave, then I said one other thing. "I am not sure what Earth has to offer; Dorn told me it is a beautiful place. I was told when I was on Boldlygo that the people are human. I feel some will not make it. Please believe me, I will do everything in my power to see that you make it to Earth. When you return to your duty, remember: Kalean is out there. He has only one objective, which is to destroy us. We must destroy him first. Please carry on with your night; I will return to my quarters."

I walked through the crowd to the corridor. In my thoughts, I felt me and my crew will never see Ticoru again. Yet, we must keep striving to do what we must—I will always hope for the best and expect the worst.

My night was long. I must say I did not sleep very much; I stared out of the window what seemed all night. Standing at the portal, I do not know why I said it, but I said, "Show yourself." There was nothing. Then, like magic, a light to the outside wall appeared. It seemed to grow bigger. My thought was this should be interesting. A portal opened and a woman stepped through. My body went flat against the wall. I do remember seeing this when Zin took me to Boldlygo; Hannah came to me once, but there was no portal.

I tried to speak, I really did. Words would not come; my mouth would not work. Shortly after she appeared, the shock had worn off. "Who are you?" I asked.

She said, "My name is not important, Paxton. King Zin sent me here; he is also my father—I am Theia. Paxton, according to our timekeeper, we cannot interfere with your destiny. We can tell you to beware. Some of your crew will not make it—Paxton, do not let this alarm you; it is their time. Some will be lost in space; some will be lost on Earth to live out their life. When the time comes, you will destroy this enemy of yours then take your place in the pod to Earth. When you reach the floor of the planet, you will be in a land called Russia." Well, I thought, where had I heard that before? "In your escape, you must find someone—two females, Mimi and Sophia. It is destiny for you to meet them. You will be taken to the home of their aunt, and there you must wait."

A portal started to open. I said, "Wait, then what?" She turned, smiling and looking at me with those crystal blue eyes. She said, "You will see."

I sat hard on the bed. My crew—some dead; some stranded on a planet we knew nothing about; me on a strange world looking for someone I did not know—so many thoughts ran through my head. I took my tea, took a sip, and laid on the bed. Somewhere in the early morning, I fell asleep for a brief time.

Morning came as it is in space; in a daze, I opened my eyes. What was happening? There was a hard knock on my door. Rolling to one side, I tried to clear my thoughts. I could not comprehend what was happening; I felt as if I had too much ale. I staggered to the door; opening the door, Mora stood smiling. Mora looked past my shoulder to see if I was alone.

I asked Mora, "Something I can help you with?"

Mora said, "Captain, are we still departing?"

I did not know what was happening. I said, "Mora, I just got to sleep."

Mora said to me, "Captain, it is almost half past the day." I told her you should have called to me; you had no problem doing that at school. "Yes, I know; but you were not the captain." I told her, "Let me dress; I will meet you on the bridge."

Mora said, "Very well, captain. I will inform the bridge." I had no idea what today would bring. In this moment, I only knew now: I washed my face, changed, and went to the bridge. Walking down the corridor, I thought of but one thing: Where was Kalean?

I had no clue; maybe hidden in an asteroid field, yet the charts did not show one. That was something Dorn and Bota told me: always stay in charted air space. I would like to think I have done that. Well, you know there has been a few exceptions. Entering the bridge, the crew was at their stations. Jabel, Rove, and Mora looked as I took my chair.

Mora asked, "Captain, shall we get underway?" I knew we had been here above Mars for several days. Looking around and taking a deep breath, I said, "Rove, take us to earth; stay cloaked."

Rove replied, "As you wish, captain." The big ship came alive. It trembled just a little then started into the darkness of space. I told Rove to travel at a normal speed; moving through space at a high speed could leave a vapor trail. I surely did not want Kalean to pick up on that. I really was in no hurry; I wanted to arrive on Earth in one peace. I was not sure what I would find on Earth—hell, I did not know why I was going to Earth. Maybe it was just my curiosity, or the fact that from the time I left the Moon of Spores—and even my brief time on Boldlygo—I was informed to go to Earth. Look where I have gone; where I have been. My parents would be proud of their son—this I do believe.

Along the way during my travels, I have met some astonishing people and other species. I have seen and been on several different planets. Some of them were rich in trade; some not so much. Some had advance in technology beyond belief. In my dreams I have met people; some come to me that way. In my thoughts—some I could not believe—this last one I had, I decided to keep to myself. I cannot or will not reveal it to my crew.

Shaking my head and bringing myself back to reality, I watched Rove at the controls as the ship moved through the dark, empty space. We were moving at a good and relevant speed. If we could continue to move without trouble, we could be in the earth's atmosphere in less than a month.

Sitting and watching the screen, it dawned on me that some of them would die, while some of them will live the rest of their lives on a planet they knew nothing about. They would need to survive somehow; I only knew they were intelligent enough to do anything they wish. Thiea did say it was their time. I was sorry for that. Everyone dies; even on Boldlygo. I know in my heart I will never live to be that old. We do grow old on Ticoru, yet we die, too.

From my chair I watched the screen for what seemed hours—there were nothing out there but space and stars; stars that shined for what seemed forever. It was like a never-ending story. What was always a mystery is if you could get close to a star, it still would look as far off as it does now.

As we traveled from a different planet, there were always different stars, yet they were all the same. Stars were just pockets of gas. Some were planets suspended in space in different galaxies; they also could be asteroids that surrounds a planet. I was at peace; I was at home in space—nothing and no one would ever keep me from traveling into the darkness and the unknown regions of space. Dorn. Zin, and Cavota told me of other planets they were allied to. The one I wanted to see and visit was the one called Eden. I also would like to visit Advair, Galaxo, Gara, and Bangor—all of them.

I was told the stories of the planets destroyed by the small group led by Zin and Shila. Maybe someday I will see them, also. I have no reason not to see them. I had only one commitment and on this I would fall short—I was the leader of the crew. I knew some of them would die; I knew also I would not have a ship on Earth. I was told humans did not do long space travel. They tried once an establishment on Mars, which failed. One would believe Earth would have advanced farther than they are. I mean, look at Bota. Bota said his first time on Earth was—oh my, that was an awfully long time ago! I thought, how old was Bota? If I ever see him again, I will ask that question. I suppose you could say Earth is what we call primitive.

I know on Ticoru, we have had space travel over five hundred years. It is as Bota said: it is in out DNA; it is in our blood. I was not sure who constructed our first ship, this was never covered in school. I suppose it really does not matter, as some would say it is now that we live for. I do know there are some highly intelligent people on my home world.

Suddenly, my thoughts went out of the ship, traveling like the machine I was in. I was traveling at the speed of light, sometimes many times faster. How fast can a mind travel? Could thoughts be registered as speed? I think not, but it was amazing how fast one could travel in one's mind, going from one place to another. If a ship could travel that fast, that would be incredible. I wonder how humans calculate speed or distance. Was this a universal measure? My ship is very capable of light speed and beyond; I do not wish to travel that fast. I also notice we do not age as fast as the beings on the planets I have visited. The ones on Boldlygo are remarkable at this; look at Dorn, and Leah, for example: Dorn is several hundreds of years older than Leah. Leah told me she was over four-hundred-years old. Trust me, she looks as young as my mother.

Mora calling to me brought be back to myself; I had no clue where I was in my thoughts. Jumping as she called to me as if I were frighten, I looked around to gather my thoughts.

Mora said, "Captain, there is a blimp on the screen." Focusing on the screen, I saw what she was pointing to. The blimp was still; it was sitting along in the darkness of space.

Mora said, "Well, it is gone just as it appeared."

I answered, "Well Mora, maybe it was a false reading, yet maybe it was something else; let us keep alert."

I wanted nothing in my way to stop me—the closer I come to Earth, the more I wanted it. More than once I have been told Earth would not give us a warm welcome; this I did not understand. I suppose I must find this out for myself. First, I had to arrive there. Since leaving Ticoru, I have enjoyed meeting others—except for Kalean. I know when we arrive—if we make it alive—I will be cautious.

We continued our journey. I told the crew to stay alert. The day as it was ended with no problem. Each moment without a problem, we were coming closer to Earth. I excused myself. I told Mora she had the bridge. I had been on the bridge since rising; I wanted a cup of tea and maybe cake. Gathering my things, I walked to a table by the big portal. I watched the ship as it traveled at a moderate speed. Suddenly, my thoughts went to the night Hannah appeared to me. It was extremely hard for me to believe someone could do this. I do know that people had powers beyond me. Hannah told me her mother could go anywhere she wanted; she also said Shila had been to Earth.

The girls told me that the humans on Earth were not as we are; they are a different kind of human. Shila told me they would not accept me. Shila said I know this because I have seen this; I have been there. Of course, Dorn told me the same—therefore, I was not sure why I was going there. I suppose just to say I have been there, or was it just the thrill of being in space? I did enjoy seeing and being in different universes and galaxies. Since I was a small child, accompanied by my father to another world, I knew this was something I have always wanted to do. Well, you know I got the chance. Yet, like my father, I would give it up—but not today.

When I was on Boldlygo, all the people that lived there said they never wanted to return to Earth; they told me they found peace and solitude on Boldlygo. I do know all the natives loved them very much. I do know the time I spent with them will always be a time I will never forget—living on Boldlygo would be a life like no other.

The beings on the planet were so intelligent, it was beyond belief. It was said their creator placed it in their DNA.

I am not sure how this works—I am not stupid, yet I am not that intelligent. I mean think about it: a man can create a portal to step from one world to another in seconds. I tell you that is extreme power. I was told Zin was the one with the greatest power. Well, I say, more power to the people.

Cavota told me once that Leah and the girls, known as the three, can and have taken on armies. Honestly, I do believe that. Toko told me about the time they came to his planet. They were pissed off, to quote Toko. Royce was the ruler of that quadrant at the time and the girls killed several hundred of his followers.

I had finished my tea when Jabel called for me to come to the bridge quickly. Hurrying down the corridor to the bridge, I thought Kalean had found us, and I was right. I was not worried, as we were still in stealth mode. I was so thankful to Cavota for installing that. Cavota is a great person. He took us, me and my crew, in as protective custody; it was a great feeling to know we were safe. Cavota was someone I really would not want to have on a bad side.

I told Rove to bring the ship to a stop and to stay cloaked.

Mora said, "Captain, from the index it is Kalean's ship; they're closing fast." I told Rove to move the ship to starboard. "Move well out of range of the path." Kalean's ship moved past us at an incredible speed. Kalean was looking for us and was on a path of destruction for anything. I do believe if we had been uncloaked, he would not have seen us—I knew he was headed for Earth. I am sure Kalean thought we were already on Earth. In my thoughts, I knew where he was. I told Rove to stay one light-year behind Kalean's ship. Mora kept the ship on the screen. I sent a message out to the crew; I told them to stay alert. I told them from now until we reach Earth, we would stay in battle station. I told them to feel free to move around and never venture far from their station.

My ship moved on at a mordent speed. From the star charts, I could see we were still two weeks from Earth's moon at this speed. Beyond the moon, the next place was Earth. I knew it was a fight to the death for some of the crew. I had told them to escape in the pods and when they reach Earth, if they were able to, take all the technology from the pods; bury it but not around where you land. I was sorry for my crew; the only thing I knew for sure is I would survive. My shift had ended. I told Jabel to call me if there was trouble.

Jabel replied, "Yes captain, as you wish." I knew it was only a matter of time before we encountered Kalean. I knew we had no choice. I do wish Zin would intervene. Why should he? It was not his fight.

Kalean's ship kept moving through space for another week. A call from the bridge brought me from the galley. Entering the bridge, Mora had this strange look on her face.

I asked, "What is wrong, Mora?" She pointed at the screen. A bright star showed ahead of us.

"Mora," I asked, "What is it and how far is it?"

Mora said, "Captain, I do believe it is a moon or it is Earth." Kalean's ship had come to a stop. Well, I knew what that meant: Kalean was waiting to plot his attack. Soon, this will be over for us. I took a quick look around. No one had any idea what was going to happen. I spoke to the crew; I told them to go to battle stations. Rove and Jabel had this look on their face.

Mora asked, "Captain, you know something we don't." I only told them to be ready. Mora was right; it was the moon. From the position we were approaching, I could not see what was on the other side.

Mora said, "The way the charts read, the other side of the moon is Earth." I only knew one thing: that was the largest moon I had ever seen. With the ship still in stealth mode, we approached the moon. Just beyond the far horizon of the moon was the big blue planet known as Earth. I have seen things in space before; seen planets no one on my world has. Dorn was right—nothing could compare to what I was looking at in this moment. With the earth's sun on the planet, I in my life have never witnessed such beauty as this. Earth was sitting like a big ball in space. There was a thought in my mind that said "Welcome; come as you are." Dorn was right—it was breath taking.

Mora called, "Captain, there is communication coming from Earth. They have spotted Kalean's ship." There was nothing that could be done. Earth had no space program, yet they did have missiles in space. I knew they had a space station and satellites. As we sat there in stealth, we waited to see what would happen.

Mora said, "Captain, Kalean's ship is moving toward Earth." I told Rove not to move, not even an inch. Kalean started his descent to the planet. A big blast hit Kalean's port side. It was too late: he was going through the earth's atmosphere. It was too late for them—to turn he would need to be completely clear of the earth's atmosphere.

We sat above the moon of Earth. I wondered about this place. This moon was more desolate than Mars. I thought we have come all this way and for what? I could not say. I only knew I was here; I made it this far. At least if I ever make it back to Ticoru, I could tell my story.

CHAPTER 11

FROM A DEEP SLEEP, SOMETHING BROUGHT ME TO life. There was a howling outside my window; it sounded as if something was scratching on the windowpane. I was not fully awake, so I cuddled in my blanket. I then realized what was happening. I stepped from my bed and looked through the window. The wind was blowing so hard; the scratching was the wind blowing the limbs from the small tree that grew outside. I suppose the howling was the wind blowing through the trees. Snow was piling high. The wind was blowing the snow around and it was a total whiteout. It was hard to believe how much snow had fallen during the night. It was going to be an awfully chilly day.

Tasha, Sophia, and sometimes Ivan, and I talked late into the night. Somewhere around four, I told them good night. From the great room to my room, lying on the bed, I thought in the past few weeks I had grown up. Sophia said the same. Of course, the other girls at the school called me a freak.

Looking into the mirror, I noticed my skin as I washed my face. Nina told me once my skin was so smooth it made her sick. Nina never did like me; I was so glad the bitch was gone. Thinking back years ago, I wish my mother could see me. I had grown into a beautiful young woman; a freak I was not. Maybe that is why everyone was so envious of me. Nina was beautiful; there was no doubt—she had those big blue eyes; a great body at sixteen. The one thing she did not have was a personality—and that ridiculous blonde hair! It was too bad we could not be friends.

Moving from the mirror, a shadow moved across the ceiling. It startled me and I froze. What the hell was that? I thought. Chills ran over me as if I were freezing. I tried to call for Sophia, I really did. My words was there, I just could not say them.

There was a scream from the great room that seemed to bring me out of the trance I was in. I ran into the room and saw Sophia, lying on the floor. I stood beside her and she looked dazed. Kneeling, Sophia reached out her hand to touch my face. Tears fell from my eyes as a lump came to my throat. I said, "Sophia, what is wrong?" From Sophia's mouth came a whisper, yet it was not her voice I heard.

The voice said, "My beloved daughter—you have grown well, Mimi. Follow Sophia. Soon, you will go on a long journey. Soon, my daughter, you will go home." I had no clue what to say or what was happening. Sophia's hand fell from my face as Tasha stood over us—it was my first time seeing her out of that big chair.

Tasha said, "Mimi, give me your hand." I found it extremely hard to lift my arm. There were thoughts running through me, like maybe I am a freak. Tasha said to me it was my mother talking to me through Sophia.

I said, "Bullshit, Tasha. How is that possible? My mother has been dead for several years." I saw a small, thin line of a smile form from the corner of her mouth.

"Come child," Tasha said. I started to stand, trying to help Sophia from the floor. Finally, Sophia told me to let her lie there for a few minutes.

Tasha made her way to the big chair, telling me to come sit by her on the sofa. I did not want to leave Sophia on the floor; I told Tasha I would as soon as I get Sophia off the floor. Looking at Tasha, I told her when I get Sophia off the floor, we are going to have a damn long talk. "Tasha, I damn well mean it." I saw another small smile come from her face.

Sophia had gained some of her strength back. She was still in somewhat of a daze. Looking at Tasha, Sophia said something in a language I did not understand.

I said, "Speak English or Russian, please."

I asked, "Sophia, what the hell happened?" Sophia began telling me of the shadow moving across the ceiling. "Then like a rock, it knocked me to the floor. Damn, I have never experienced anything like that."

Tasha said, "For many years, I have watched that shadow move. I have never said a word. It was your mother, Mimi. She was waiting for the right time. This was her time to act; she had to tell you goodbye. That is all I can say."

Sophia asked, "Did she say anything to you, Mimi?" Look, I do not know what is happening here. I do know the shit I have seen is real. Tasha said it was my mother.

Sophia asked again, "Mimi, did she say anything to you?"

I said, "She told me to follow you. She said I would be going on a journey, that I would be going home. My home is here with you and Tasha. Do not misunderstand: I do love the school. I love Tasha; I love this house. Sophia, I love you deeply. I love being here. Today, this morning scared the hell out of me. You know if I knew what to expect, it would not bother me so. It is as if there is a different surprise every day. I tell you it is more than I can comprehend, yet it happens."

Walking to the kitchen for tea, I turned to ask if anyone wanted tea. Glancing at Tasha, she was asleep—or she appeared to be. Sophia shook her head no.

Looking through the window, the snow was falling fast and so hard you could not see. The wind whipped the snow from the ground, like feathers blowing. It was causing a complete whiteout. The temperature was sitting at zero. In my lifetime, I have never witnessed a winter such as this.

Sophia finally stood, walking to the television and turning it to the news. It was the first time that thing had been turned on. She said she wanted to hear the weather forecast. Sitting by Tasha, I listened to the newsman. Tasha took Sophia's arm and said, "Sophia, they are here." The reporter said, "This just in." I was curious of what he had to say. The man said, "An object has been spotted in the earth's atmosphere."

I started to shake again. "Who is here, Sophia?" I asked. Sophia looked at me with those crystal blue eyes.

Sophia replied, "I think you already know that answer, Mimi."

Tasha looked at me and said, "Soon Mimi, it will be over. I tell you this. Keep your thoughts open and clear. Mimi, Sophia; always remember I love you both." Tasha reached out her hand. Sophia took one while I took the other. I swear, every hair on my body stood out; I had a sensation like I have never felt before. The feeling rushed through me like water over a dam. I looked at Sophia; she had her eyes closed and every hair on her was moving as if wind was blowing it around. Ivan was standing in the doorway, saying I feel it, too.

I looked at Tasha, lying in her big chair with her eyes closed and a smile on her face. Then it had dawned on me: Sophia had tears falling down her face, and so did I. Tasha left this world; it is something I do not wish to face again. Sophia and I stood and kissed Aunt Tasha on the cheek. I told Sophia I felt Tasha had so much to tell me.

Ivan said, "What do I do now? I have been with Tasha most of my life. I am not her blood, yet I was her son."

Looking over at Sophia, she was crying and sobbing so hard. I tell you the three of us were a mess. There was so much more I wanted to know; so much unsaid. Sophia was walking around the room. Sophia said, "You know Tasha loved this room; it was her home in Saint Petersburg."

I asked Sophia, "Where did Tasha get her money?"

Sophia said, "Well, she owned the school. The Russian government paid her some. Then she had other things she was into. I do remember her telling the stories way back with Comp and Lola. It was said that each time the star people appeared—that is what they were called—each time they came, they would give Tasha a bag of stones." I thought, whatever.

Ivan said he would take care of this. He would call the authorities. Sophia told us we would wait to go through Tasha's things. "Let us wait until she is taken from the house." We needed to see what we could do; try if we could to make since of it all. Sophia said since I was the legal heir, all of it was mine. I did not know what to say—I was sixteen. For the first time in my life, I had something. I owned a house and so much more. Sophia had calmed down and so had I.

Sipping our tea, the question came back to money. Sophia told me again of Tasha's stories. "Each time the star people would come, they would pass a bag of stones to Tasha. It was said on the planet of Boldlygo you did not need money; whatever you wanted was there. Only what the planet had to offer. Trust me Mimi, the stories were the best." I asked, "Then what about the stones?"

"Well, Mimi, from what Tasha told me in her stories, the stones were everywhere—in their rivers, streams, in their yards—everywhere. There was one exception: you could not leave the planet with them. Zin had seen to that. Only him, Dorn, Leah, and a few others were able to do so. If you were caught trying, Zin would ban you from the planet. Trust me, no one ever did except one person—a couple that took their son and lived in New Mexico; they started a trade route with Zin. To this day it still exists; it's there, waiting for them to return someday. I do believe there was a captain of a ship who was the last to come here. Now each time they came here, stones were left. However, I am not sure how many stones were left. I am not sure when they came, but Tasha said they did come often.

"I have read some of the stories, Mimi, but not all of them. Tasha placed several books in old trunks upstairs. I think it would take several months to read them all if you read them in order. Tomorrow I will show you everything Tasha showed me."

I looked over to Ivan. "Did Tasha show you these books and other things?" I asked.

Ivan said, "Tasha showed me everything. She told me the stories often. Believe me, each time there was a different one. Girls, I am not sure how she knew the things she knew; it was as if she was there. In my heart, I think she was at one time. I only tried to love and take care of her; I would like to think I did. Tasha took me in when I was eight years old; I was her nephew. I have been with her since. She took me off the streets; sent me to school. She gave me a home—I was thankful for that. I am the one that found you." I looked at Ivan fast. "Tasha told me to search for you. How she knew there was another family member here, I cannot say. I searched each orphanage until I found you. It was not hard to spot you—I saw you one night using your powers that you did not even know you had. I told Tasha where you were. Mimi, before coming here from Saint Petersburg, I was with Tasha the day she let Mayrra go. It was the hardest thing she had ever had to do. Trust me, she was sad for a long time. Believe me Mimi, I believe you will be leaving soon. Sophia will go with you."

Sophia asked, "Young lady, would you like to hear more?" Well, I was for that. So, I smiled and said: "Yes."

Sophia started telling the stories all the way back to the first time the star man came to Earth. It was so long ago. It would seem they have come to Earth since. The star man came alone several times, then one day he brought a female and left her with a man and woman. Even then, he passed stones to him. The woman was with a child—that is what started the earth family. "Sophia, I had a dream about that place. It is in the country of Georgia. That is where Hannah came to me. Remember Sophia? That is when the bitch broke my finger." Sophia busted out with a loud laugh.

Sophia said, "I remember you running into a wall crying like a baby."

I jumped up, "Sophia, do not make me kick your ass." That made us laugh harder. That night, Sophia and I made a bond between us that was stronger than ever. Sophia and I sat in silence for a while. I broke the silence by asking what Tasha meant when she said they are here.

Sophia said, "The object in the earth's atmosphere—well Mimi, it is a ship."

I asked, "What about the one we saw at the school?"

Sophia said, "I am not sure about that one, Mimi. You did say in this dream we were supposed to meet someone." I told Sophia that Hannah did say that the only thing I am sure of is this. "Sophia, how does one find a person from another world on Earth? Think about it, who are they? How do they look? Where is this to take place? We could sit here all night or forever without knowing who they are."

Sophia said, "Mimi, it will all work out in time; you will see." Well, I left it at that. Sophia and I joined Ivan in the next room. Ivan told us he had made the arrangements for Tasha. Ivan told Sophia if she liked, we could start tomorrow going through Tasha's things. Sophia and I agreed, then we made a small meal and talked awhile. Dishes were done, and I said good night then walked to my room. I did not take a bath; I changed into my sleeping clothes. I walked to the window to watch the snow fall—I was trying to clear my thoughts by gazing into the night sky and watching the snowflakes come down. In the mist somewhere above the earth was a huge light as I have never seen before, then it was as if hundreds of small lights streaked through the sky. I ran to the great room told Sophia.

Sophia said, "I know Mimi, I saw them too." I went back to my room and walked straight to the window. For some reason, the snow had stopped and the sky was clear. Stars twinkled in the sky like diamonds. In my life looking into the heavens, I do not remember seeing so many stars. I saw what appeared to be a shooting star. I turned to go back to my bed when the sky lit up again with thousands of lights. It was like an explosion in the sky.

It was something to see. The Russian air force was flying everywhere. Something flashed by in the clear night sky. I promise you, it was like nothing I have seen before— and it was fast. It was as big as the town of Vologda; lights bounced of it like bombs were being fired at it. I watched it as it started to climb high into the darkness of the sky. Thousands of feet above the earth it disappeared, as if it was never there.

In my thoughts I knew what it was. I knew it was a UFO, I was sure of it. I think the Russian air force believed it, too. There were over a hundred planes in the air; they flew over the house all night. I watched and listen for a while, then sleep overtook me. Walking to my bed, I fell asleep. It was as if I just got to sleep when Sophia touched my arm. Turning to see her, it was not Sophia.

I said, "Damn, can you come to me when I am awake? What now, Hannah?"

Hannah said, "If I come to you when you are awake, where would the fun be in that, Mimi?" I raised up in bed and told Hannah I would kick her ass.

Hannah said, "Oh Mimi, not on your best day. You are not that strong in your powers yet." Hannah told me to rise. I sat cross legged on the bed as Hannah told me I would soon meet the captain of this ship. "What you saw tonight was a ship entering the earth's atmosphere. The ship you saw has left Earth and has returned to space. In a brief time, that ship will encounter the ship controlled by Paxton, the captain. There will be only a few that will survive."

I said, "Well Hannah, if you or your king is all powerful, why can you not stop this?"

Hannah said, "We cannot interfere; it is their time. Soon you will meet this captain, after all is done."

I asked, "How am I to know this person, Hannah?" Hannah turned to me, then someone called and she was gone. It seemed I had just closed my eyes when Sophia called to me. "Mimi, come to the great room, please." My thought was what is wrong with these people? I am on a break from school—leave me the hell alone. I placed my robe around me while looking out the window—damn, it was full day. I thought I had fallen back to sleep after the visit from Hannah.

Sophia said, "Young lady we have a big day today. Since the snow has stopped, we need to go where Tasha is. Ivan has said he has made the arrangements, however Tasha wanted to be cremated. We will take care of that, then return here with Ivan to start going through Tasha's belongings. We will need to work hard since school starts back in six days." I knew this would be hard on the three of us, but it was something that had to be done. When we started, I could not believe how much stuff Tasha had. Tasha was old for a human; she had a long time to accumulate things. I do believe her most prized possessions were the books of the family—these she kept in an old trunk locked away.

Having a light breakfast, we drove to the place where Tasha laid. Sophia did what she had to do. We made it back home just as the snow started to fall again—it was coming down hard. This time it was mixed with sleet, and that meant it would be icy.

Sophia said as she closed the door of the car: "Damn Mimi, it is cold." Running for the steps, Sophia slid. I kind of snickered. Sophia said, "If I fall, I will kick your ass, Mimi." I really laughed out loud, and while running up the steps I asked Sophia, "Why do we need to go back to school?"

Sophia said, "So you can learn, dummy." Going through the door, I grabbed Sophia around the waist; we hit the floor as we rolled into Ivan coming through the door.

Ivan said, "Having fun, girls?" We said at the same time, "Yes!" The three of us worked hard going through Tasha's things. Six hours passed before we decided to take a break. Just before Sophia stopped, she pulled out a drawer from the dresser that fell apart. A large bag fell to the floor. Sophia picked it up and it made a jingle sound. Sophia looked at me and Ivan to say, "What is this?" Suddenly a strange feeling came over me: I could read every thought that ran through Sophia's mind. I was sitting on the floor, then suddenly I fell over, shaking and turning the color of the clouds. Sophia picked me up, calling to me. Opening my eyes I said, "What happened?" Sophia started to explain. I told her I thought I was dying.

"Sophia," I said, "I could read every thought you were thinking. Sophia, what is happening to me?" Sophia said to me she was not sure. Sophia helped me to the bed; she picked up the bag and opened it up. She told me it was full of stones. I knew this was something I have read about and what Sophia had told me. Sophia poured them out on the bed. I tell you they were precious stones—it was like nothing on this Earth. From starman to my mother, Tasha, it said; each time they brought stones, give them to the earth family.

Ivan looked at us and asked, "Do you girls want me to leave or stay?" I told him he was not going anywhere. Sophia told him he was staying. "We will need someone to watch the place when we are not here. Remember, Ivan: you are family too. Things will not change. You have been with Tasha for an exceedingly long time."

We were excited about the stones. We took a break for tea. I picked up a folded piece of paper when the drawer fell apart. Opening the paper, I looked at Sophia. I started to hand it to Sophia.

Sophia said, "You can read it?" I told Sophia it was long. She replied, "We're not going anywhere."

"*It has been a long time since words were wrote. As of now, I have no one for my estate. I was born in the year twenty-one sixty-five.*" I thought Tasha was ninety years old—that was old for a person on Earth. The pages were turning yellow. "*I only have Ivan; he is ten and my brother's son. I was told of a young woman that lives in Moscow; I will check this out soon.*"

"*I took Ivan off the street. I did not know of him since my brother and I had different opinions. He lives with me; Ivan is young but can do most anything. I will send him to school to further his education. I do have people searching through the villages and towns, trying to find if my family is alive. Today, so far, no one has come. If I cannot find a member of the earth family, I will leave it all to him.*" I asked Sophia about this. She told me it was before her time or mine. I looked at Ivan, I told him he would be taken care of. I told him he would live here as before—nothing will change. Sophia started to read again.

"*I have sold everything in Saint Petersburg and I will take Ivan to Moscow. I will let the other people know that work for me where to find me. When Ivan grows older, he will do the same. I moved here to Moscow after my beloved Mayrra left. Whoever finds this, remember I love Ivan, but Mayrra was special. She had her own kind of powers.*" I stopped Sophia. "So Shila is real?"

Sophia said, "Apparently, she is."

"Damn, Sophia, this just keeps getting better. Somehow I thought the dreams were just that. This bullshit is still hard to believe."

"*A young woman came to the house today—the same one that was in Moscow. I knew her as soon as I saw her. Opening the door, I addressed her and said 'Come in Sophia, I have been waiting on you. In fact, I have waited for a long time.' Sophia stood in the door with her mouth open. Sophia said, 'Who are you?' I told her I was Tasha, her aunt. I told her to come in; we have things to talk about. Soon after several visits, she accepted her that her fate had been dealt. Her and Ivan grew as brother and sister—that was fine for me.*

"*I got Sophia a position at the school today; I mean after all, I did own the school. I gave her several books of the family. Sophia, in order for you to know what is going on in the family's life, you must read them—each word. She agreed. Several weeks had passed when she came to me and brought back the books. I give her a test to see if she really did read them, and she passed. Sophia said to me, 'Tasha, it is hard for me to believe what I have read. In my heart, I do believe it is true.'*

"*From time-to-time, Sophia would come to the house. She would stay sometimes overnight. If there was no school, she would stay for a while. She would ask questions about the stars and about the family. Of course, I had first class information. Meeting Shila and Fina once, and others would stop in when they came to Earth. Zin came to me after Mayrra left; he has come several times. Zin told me I could come home if I wanted to. I always said to him there are others here for them so I must decline; this was before Sophia came here.*

I DON'T BELONG HERE

"One day after Sophia left for school, another caller came to the house and Ivan let him in. He was a man I had working for me. I had employed him to check something out. He told me he had found someone I might be interested in; he said her mother and father had passed. He told me the child was in an orphanage for girls. Her name was Mimi."

I looked at Sophia as the tears fell down my face. Sophia smiled as if to say I love you. *"I had the car brought around, and I told Ivan to come with me. Ivan drove me to the school where I met with Mimi—she was six at the time."*

I said, "Wait, I do remember that! That was almost eleven years ago." Sophia kept reading. "The child was so beautiful. She reminded me of Mayrra. She had the family hair and eyes. Looking like Mayrra did help me make up my mind—Mayrra was so beautiful; I watched her grow until she was old enough to leave. Later, Zin came to me told me the things Mayrra had accomplished, and I was so proud of her.

"Time comes and time goes. I sent Sophia to the home where Mimi stayed. 'Sophia,' I said, 'she will be strong. I can see this. Mimi will grow in time and she will learn to do the things she was meant to do. Then Mimi will go home to the stars—you will see.' I am not sure if Sophia will go with her or if she will stay on Earth—that decision will be hers. If I am still among the living, I will insist on her going. If I have passed and she finds this, Sophia: do not stay on Earth. Go with Mimi; leave it all to Ivan. He should retain a good life with the stones that Zin brought me through his portal.

"Mimi has grown into a beautiful young woman; she has had a good life. I have made sure of that. I am glad she has grown—Mimi will need it on her journey. Today will be my last entry. I would love to see what lies beyond the stars, but I am too old to make that journey. Sophia will take control for me now and after I pass."

I looked over to Sophia; she had tears streaming from her blue eyes, and so did I.

I said, "Sophia, I do wish I could have come sooner; I will miss her." The three of us continued to move Tasha's things from the closet. Tasha did not have much, just some old cloths. In the attic was a different story—there were several old trunks filled with small and large books. These were the books of the family. Sophia told us we would go through them tomorrow.

Sophia asked, "Mimi, what do you think about the message Tasha said about Ivan?"

I said, "Sophia, what I have learned and read in the few books is that if I go on this journey, I will not need anything. You and Ivan can have it; I am fine with that."

Sophia said, "Young lady, you are not going anywhere without me. It is done—I am coming with you. Who knows, maybe I will find a place to live; maybe have a child someday. I might teach schools there about Earth."

I ask, "Well, will that be on Boldlygo or Galaxo?" Sophia told me she was not sure; maybe she would go farther. We both laughed.

The day had slipped away. Outside the snow had stopped. It was a blustery day; snow piled high on the stoop. Ivan had shoveled it so we could maybe go down the high steps. I thought, why one would want to go out?. Sophia and I started to make a small meal. Ivan had returned from the stoop. In the great room, Ivan was looking out the window when someone knocked on the door. Ivan started to the door. I looked from the kitchen to see Russian police standing outside, then Ivan opened it.

"May I come in?" he asked. Ivan looked at me. The way the wind was blowing the snow around, I nodded my head—I wondered what would bring this man out in such awful weather. Ivan told him to enter and to please shake the snow from your boots. He said his name was Yuri. Ivan watched as I made my way around the table. Sophia asked what was is nature for the calling? He said he was from the Moscow police station. Sophia looked a little disturbed. Sophia spoke to me without moving her mouth. I shook my head as I watched him.

I asked, "Sir, what can we do for you on such a night?"

He asked, "The old woman who lives here—where is she, did she go on a trip?" Sophia told him she had passed. "I am her niece;" then pointing at me, Sophia told him I was her great niece.

Yuri said, "I see. I am sorry for the loss. I was wondering about her. I was here long ago; I am sorry to say I never returned."

Sophia said, "Well, Tasha has lived here for several years. How long has it been for you?" Yuri started talking about some young people that lived her long ago. They suddenly left after we started our investigation. It was said they were not from here—I knew right away who he was talking about.

I said, "I have no idea what you are saying. I found out Tasha was my aunt several months ago. You said the people that lived her were not from here. Where were they from? Where did they go?" I could tell he was pissed off.

Yuri said, "They escaped through the border of Ukraine; it was said they had powers of some kind." I started to laugh and this really pissed him off. He slapped the counter with both hands. Sophia stood beside me.

Sophia said, "Sir, it is time for you to leave. You come to my home and disrespect me and my family."

Yuri said, "I can have a team come here and tear this place apart. You are a child, one that needs to learn her place." Sophia told him to call whomever he liked. "Before they can arrive, I will mess you up." Ivan came through the door. "Sophia, what is going on?" Sophia explained. Ivan walked to the door and said, "Sir, it is time for you to leave." "Or what?" Yuri said.

Ivan replied, "I asked you kindly to leave; now I am telling you to get the hell out." Walking to the door, Yuri looked back and said: "I will be back." Snow was falling so hard, it had piled high on the stoop and steps. Yuri took a step and with my help fell on his ass all the way down. Smiling, I thought, good enough for the asshole. Sophia and I made our plates and went to the table.

Sophia said, "You see Mimi, this is why I will be going with you." It is none of the Moscow police's business what we do. They can kiss my ass.

I said, "Well Sophia, they can kiss your ass; maybe they will leave my ass alone." We both laughed loudly. Ivan shook his head.

Throughout the night the snow fell, in my life on this Earth, I have never seen snow fall the way it has. I could not believe how high it had piled. Tasha's house from the street was fourteen steps to the stoop and it was up to the top step. I guess you could say we were snowed in. Looking through the huge window, there was nothing moving; no animals, no birds—nothing. The clouds had started to break up; a plane would fly over every now and then. The wind was blowing so hard, I was glad to be inside. I went to the bathroom then to the kitchen where Sophia was cooking something.

Sophia said, "Good morning, young lady. You could have slept in." I told her I had been awake for a while. I inquired about the school.

Sophia said, "Mimi, I am not sure what will happen. I will be glad when all of this is over." I said the same. Off to the west, the clouds started to build again. Ivan came in and said it had started to snow again. I told him I was not surprised. The three of us spent the day talking and going through Tasha's things. Now and then, we would break to look outside. All day, nothing moved. We spent the next three days going through Tasha's things until it was done. We kept the books out so I could read them. I asked Ivan if he would like to keep them. He said whatever I wanted him to do, he would do.

Ivan said, "I will keep them until I pass. Sophia, I know you and Mimi are leaving, so I will keep what you leave. What happens to the things after I am gone, I cannot say. I think Tasha would have wanted this." Sophia said the same.

The first of the year was coming. Since the horrific snow storm, the snow started to melt. Sophia said, "Mimi, we must try to go to school." One more week we stayed, then on a Sunday evening we departed, leaving Ivan with the house.

Sophia and I were making a meal. Well, I watched—she was making lamb chops. It was absolutely my favorite dinner meat. Most children did not like lamb chops, but I was not one of them. Sophia had the pan good and hot. Ivan ran into the house. "Sophia, come quick—you too, Mimi." We ran behind Ivan, not knowing what we were to see or find. Stopping on the back stoop, Ivan said, "Look up." In the clear evening sky, just before dark and ten thousand feet above, sat a UFO.

I said out loud, "Damn, they have found me." Sophia laughed out loud. There was no mistaking it; it was as clear as the night. The Russian air force was all over it. The thing turned skyward and moved off until it was consumed by the darkness of space.

I said, "Well, they know we are here." Sophia led the way back to the kitchen. Heating the pan up, she made the chops—I must say they were delicious. We were not talking much at the table; I could tell Sophia had something on her mind. Ivan was quiet also. As for me, I was thinking about what was going to happen next. That thought did not take long—something shook the big house like an earthquake. I jumped from my chair and ran to the big window with Sophia, and Ivan beside me. The entire world seemed to light up.

Sophia said, "I think they are back."

I said, "Now what, Sophia?" She told me she was ready to get back to school. Two days later, that is what we did. I thought this was a good thing; I wanted to see the other girls—the ones that would come back to school anyway. Driving into the school yard, it all looked the same. Going inside, all the girls were there. I looked around to see if Nina was there—I did not see her and I was glad for that. As they say, when one door closes, another one opens; the good with the bad follows. It had come to be quite a little school for girls; to a school in the middle of Khimki. It was that damn policeman, Yuri. He had come to our school, my school. He was with the caretaker I saw when Sophia and I left for the holidays. I had no clue who he was, but I was about to find out.

Yuri open the door and walked in as if he owned the school. Yuri never announced himself; the girls standing by the door yelled out. Sophia had gone to her study to place down her things. When the girls yelled out, she came running in to the room.

Sophia asked, "What is going on in here?" One of the girls pointed; turning, Sophia saw Yuri. Sophia said, "Do you have a habit of walking in to a girl's school? What if they were not dressed?"

Yuri yelled, "I am Russian police; I do as I wish." Sophia looked at me as before and I read every thought in her mind. I said to her without moving my mouth: I am ready, give me a reason. Sophia said with a strong voice, "I do not care what you are or who you are. You never enter this school again without identifying yourself. This is a school for girls."

The man with Yuri said, "This is a school for dad girls. You have hurt my brother's daughter; you will be punished for this." He started to speak, but I stopped him. "You are talking about Nina, is that right? Let me tell you this. Nina has been in several schools around Moscow and has been kicked out of all of them. Nina is a damn bully. My name is Mimi; I kicked you precious Nina's ass. I will do it again if she returns, this I promise you. If you leave now, I won't kick your ass. I am asking you to leave." Yuri stood in between us. "Yuri, you were at my aunt Tasha's home last week. We told you we went to school here; I have been here for nine years. Sophia is the school mom; she teaches us every day. There is nothing going on here that should not be going on. Yuri, you need to go—we have broken no Russian law. Nina is the bad one. You may give her a message from me."

Yuri asked, "What would that be?"

I said, "Tell Nina never to come here again." I walked to the door and opening it, I said, "Now get the hell out of this school before you piss me off. Sir, if you do not leave, I will contact the commandant and report you and your friends for harassment." Yuri saw it was over. Yuri walked to the door with his friend. Walking into the chilly air, he slipped on the ice and fell on his ass. I smiled—good enough for him.

Time comes and goes. For the next several weeks, things went well. Sophia and I were spending more time together and that was good for me. Sophia would tell me all she could and what she knew about the family. Some of the girls told me and Sophia it was good that Nina did not return; some of the girls said their lives were great. In my brain, I smiled, thinking Nina was a bitch.

Sometimes, mornings come too early. I opened my eyes to a thin gray line through the east window—that only meant one thing: the gray, early morning of dawn was coming. There was nothing I could do about it; it was as time— it waits on no one. The thing about time is it always comes and goes; it always brings you something; sometimes things you want, sometimes things you do not until it comes. Lying on my back I thought, when will all this come to a head, like that Mayrra told me? As the morning sky turned to daylight, I knew time was running out. The early morning of spring had come; the birds outside the window were singing. Most of the snow was gone except in the very shady places.

I sat to the side of the bed. Somewhere outside, I heard voices. I eased my way to the door, trying not to make a sound. I was listening, yet I heard nothing more. I opened the door and there was nothing. I walked to the rail, looking to the great room. The sun was shining through and there were two men sitting on the sofa with their back to the stairs. I thought, what is going on here? Who were these two men? I started to go down the stairs, realizing I only had my pj's on and that I had forgotten to place my robe on. I thought piss on it—I do have a nice body and this was a school for girls. I could see Sophia talking to the two men.

Sophia and the men were having a discussion. One of the men told Sophia, as he took some papers from a bag: "Sophia, you will find everything is in order just as your aunt Tasha explained to us upon her death." The other man said, "We would really like to meet Mimi." I thought this man had a very heavy Russian ascent. "Sophia, Mimi would need to sign the title." Stepping around the corner, I asked, "What title? Sophia, who are these people?"

Sophia said, "Mimi, come here." Walking around the corner, I sat next to Sophia. Looking at the two men, I could read their thoughts as it ran through their brains. If they continued to think what they were, I was going to slap the shit out of them like I did Nina. I could not believe how they stared at me—I know someone somewhere would laugh out loud if they heard that. They both were staring at my legs.

I had only been out of bed ten minutes. My long, dark hair was unbrushed and hung way past my shoulders. I had no make-up on. Tasha said I did not need it, that it was not like me; others said the same. As for myself, I never thought I was beautiful. Sophia has told me I was incredibly beautiful. I just let it pass through one ear canal and out the other side, just to drift on the wind. I was five foot two inches tall and one hundred fifteen pounds. Some of the girls here at the school said I was stacked, yet I could care less. Mother nature made me this way—there was nothing I could do about it. To me, I was just Mimi. Sophia introduced the men as Aunt Tasha's attorneys.

I said, "Good morning. What title are you talking about?"

Sophia said, "Mimi, Tasha has left everything to you. So, you will need to sign the title so all of Tasha's holdings can be transferred to you." I looked at Sophia, smiling. "Before I sign anything, I must read them. Could you leave them on the table please? I also need to discuss something with Sophia. I do hope that is not an inconvenience. You could return Friday to pick them up, and you and I could have a talk, that way you can see me again." Both men turned red; one of them started to speak when I said, "Sorry sir, I have spoken." I went back up the stairs to my room and heard the outside door close. Sophia ran up the stairs to my room.

Sophia said, "You little shit head, what was that all about?"

I said, "Sophia, you know we are leaving. To make Ivan the owner of this, we must do it legally, or the damn Russian government will take it from him."

Sophia said, "Damn Mimi, I completely forgot about that. Mimi, it has been two months since you had that dream. Hell, nothing has happened, so what do you think is going on?"

I said, "I am not sure. I do believe it will happen, but I am not sure when. When it does, Sophia, we need to be ready." I took my bottoms off and my top. I stood in just my panties, looking in the mirror. Oh, I could see why they were staring at me. I put on my jeans, shirt, and boots to go outside. I started to head for the door when the world lit up like a lightning storm.

I said, "Damn, Sophia, what was that?" Sophia was the color of the clouds, and so was I. We ran down the stairs to be with the other girls. Outside, there was a huge cloud of smoke and something exploded. Suddenly there was a flash, then something went straight up—something had destroyed a Russian plane. It was a ship, the same one as before.

Sophia said, "Damn what now?" I did not know what to say, so I stood in silence.

CHAPTER 12

MORA CALLED TO ME FROM THE BRIDGE. I WAS IN the engine room talking to my engineer. In counsel, I asked if there were a way to better protect the ship from a blast.

Jorgen said, "Captain just stay in stealth. He cannot see us, is that right?" I told him we cannot be detected in stealth. "Jorgen, the ship must not be in stealth mode to enter any planet's atmosphere."

Jorgen said, "I was there when Cavota installed it; he never said that to me."

I said, "Jorgen, I know, yet I was told by Dorn and Zin we must be clear of stealth to enter anyone's atmosphere. Jorgen, that is what I am afraid of—if Kalean is around, he will know the moment we come out of cloak, the very minute we appear." I answered Mora's call and headed back to the upper level to the bridge.

Mora said as I entered the bridge, "Captain, Kalean's ship is on the backside of Earth. When he comes around, he will be low and at risk. It appears, captain, the place has an air force. Kalean fired on one of the vessels causing it to explode—that is what we saw from above the moon; it was huge." I went to my chair; I did not wish for my crew to be in harm's way.

The way I see it, they are going to die. It will be here, there, or somewhere; it was said it was their time. My ship sat still on the top side of the moon. I told Rove to hold where we were. Standing, I told Jabel to come with me. Jabel and I walked to the launch deck. We inspected the pods, making sure they were in order. I made sure the coordinates were programed.

Returning to the bridge, I told the crew once more: "If for whatever reason I tell you to abandon ship, please do not hesitate; each of you are assigned a pod. Make sure you are in your pod. Remember, expect the worst, hope for the best. I assure you, we will do our best to make it to Earth.

"We will be coming out of stealth soon; this means Kalean will be able to detect the ship. We will enter the earth's atmosphere; hopefully all we have been through will help us prevail. Kalean has been on the back side of Earth, so I could not detect him. I watched as his ship appeared on my screen. I told Rove to stay alert. I will stay here until I see where he is. Jabel, you do exactly what I say when I say it. Jabel, go to your station and wait."

It was a long wait; longer than I expected. I knew where he was and I waited for him to make his move. Believe me, he will make it—he has been out of sight long enough. He was that way, always too anxious; wanting to make a big name for himself. If it all goes well, he will never live to tell of this day to anyone. One way or the other, me or Kalean will die.

Kalean needed to be destroyed—he lived for it and his crew, also. Earth humans, according to Dorn and Zin, will not accept them. The humans would kill them for being what they are. We sat for several hours, waiting.

Mora called to me, "Captain, he is here." "Damn," I jumped, "Where? How close?" Mora smiled, "He is coming around very slowly, captain." I looked at Jabel.

Jabel said, "Do not worry about me captain, just give me the word." I told Rove when he makes his turn to go around from us then uncloak the ship. "Jabel, then and only then fire three blasts of the cannon. While he is trying to figure out what has happened, we will hit the earth's atmosphere and descend to Earth."

Mora said, "This is why you are the captain. I like it."

I said, "Just remember what I said about the pods—do not hesitate. Hopefully, we can meet on Earth. I placed us somewhere on the charts. The pods should arrive in this area—at least I hope."

Mora watched Kalean's ship as it covered the area where the pods were to land. Rove dropped from the top

of the moon, still in stealth. We were just above the lay-
er that protected Earth. I watched on as Kalean made his
turn. I yelled, "Now, Jabel! Now!" Jabel fired three rounds
from the cannon. It was a hit into Kalean's impulse engine.
It was not where I wanted it to hit, yet it was something.
Apparently, it was not enough. "Damn," I said. I did not
expect this. Kalean made a swift turn and headed straight
toward us. Jabel fired again, hitting Kalean in the port side
below the main hull. Jabel fired yet again, hitting close to the
same place. I yelled to Rove to get us out and cloak the ship.
Kalean fired, hitting us in the starboard side. We were back
where we started. I told the crew it was no use; it won't hold
long. The cloak failed as the power dropped. Kalean made
his turn, and so did I.

Kalean came at us head on, firing at my ship. The first
round hit on the aft. This was not a direct hit; we could
survive. Jabel fired everything at once. I tell you, it was
something to see. Jabel did not destroy the ship, yet the ship
sustained heavy damage. I wanted that ship destroyed—I
wanted it destroyed in space. I could not have Kalean or my
ship falling to Earth in pieces. I knew what would happen—
the humans on Earth would die or there would be so much
damage; this would probably cause panic, not to include the
fallout from the nuclear engine.

Jabel fired several shorter bursts. Kalean fired, hitting
the ship about where the galley was. Debris and people were
pulled out into space. I knew then it was over; we could not

enter the Earth's atmosphere with this kind of damage—
the ship would be destroyed completely. I gave the order to
abandon ship. I watched as several ran for the pods. Jabel
and Mora looked at me like I am staying. I yelled "Go! Go
now!" Kalean saw this; I was sure he thought he had won.
I still had one trick—Kalean did not know I was still on the
ship.

I lined my ship with his and made a fast punch, flying
over top of his ship. It had been a long time since I had
control of the ship in my hands. The big ship did what I
asked of her. Flying fast to Kalean and just before hitting, I
pulled the controls up, flying just above him. Looking on the
screen, I saw all the pods had made it through the earth's
atmosphere. Pulling back again on the controls, I did a big
loop one thousand feet above Kalean. I was far enough to
nosedive into Kalean's ship—there was no way he could
see what was about to happen. I am sure he was wondering what was happening. At five hundred feet, I ran to my
pod. Climbing in and locking myself in, I ejected the pod
as my ship nosedived into Kalean. In the cold darkness of
space, never to harm another being, Kalean met his faith. I
watched from the portal of the pod as I blasted toward the
earth's atmosphere.

Moving through space, something hit the pod and sent
me into a spin. Looking out of the portal, I could see a piece
of debris as it bounced off the pod. I thought, on no, this
knocked me off course—how much, though, I could not say.

Dropping below ten thousand feet, everything was going crazy. The human's air force were everywhere. I was not sure what war looked like on Earth, but I thought this was it. I was afraid the air force saw me. I was not sure which way my crew went. I knew they cleared the earth's atmosphere and they made a landing somewhere to the west; how far, I could not say.

Looking through the portal, I could see the pod slowing down. Taking my hand and wiping the condensation from the window, I could see the mountains. In my thought, it looked almost like the Ticoru mountains covered with ice. I do remember looking at the mountains again before I hit the mountain at the base. In a flash, I went home in my mind, back to the Ticoru mountains; to the ice caps—how beautiful it was. Maybe this would be my last thought before I die. The ice caps would melt, giving way to the tropical valley where we lived. This was the last thing I remembered before hitting the mountain. I hit hard, knocking me unconscious.

I woke up, not knowing how long I had been out; looking through the portal, I could tell darkness had come. Before I hit, it was full light outside. I could see stars twinkling in the sky; they seemed to be millions of miles away. I suppose they were—they were light-years away. I could tell the outside was very cold; the portal window had frosted over. I opened the hatch while raising myself above it. I took in a deep breath; I could see nothing but snow. Nothing was moving, not even a flying machine—this let me know I had not been seen. I had no clue how long I had been here or what I was going to do. Before closing the hatch, I took one last look. I saw nothing, not even a light, only the chilly wind blowing the snow. Inside, I took the survival kit from the overhead, took out the blanket and wrapped it around me; somewhere in the night, I fell asleep.

From outside the pod, a noise woke me. Looking through the window portal, a flying machine was looking around. I knew it was me they were looking for; I had never seen anything like this—it had a twirling blade on top. I knew someday I would find out what this was called. Today, all I wanted to do was find where my crew was if I could. In my thoughts, I had no idea; however, I wished they were together. I know only one thing: I do not belong here. I remember Hannah telling me I would survive and that is what I have done today. For now, I must find a village or a town.

Walking down the mountain gave me time to think. How did the people on Earth purchase what they needed? Dorn and Leah told me they used money, whatever that was. I do remember Zin giving me a small gold nugget as a gift. I always kept in in my pocket. I suppose I could use that; I am sure the people of Earth have heard of gold. Walking became easier. I did not know which way to start. I saw the funny looking flying machine head to the east—that is the way I will go. The mountain turned into a vast open range that made the walking much easier. I saw nothing of a living being except for a few funny looking animals running around. I saw no tracks of people. The farther I was from the mountain and snow, the warmer it seemed.

In the distance, I could hear that funny flying machine. If it comes back, I will surely be seen. I took my jacket and spread my blanket under a bush, then sat to rest. How long I had walked, I could not say. I was thinking of all that had happened as I closed my eyes, then I seemed to drift off to a pleasant time. Opening my eyes, I thought, that did not last long. The wind had changed direction. From a distance, I caught the smell of smoke. Looking toward the sky, I thought of Kalean. I was not sure why I thought of him; the fate he got was good enough for him. He did what he had to do. Hannah told me long ago not to think about it; it was his time. Believe me, I had no regrets of taking him out. The only regret I have was my people on Earth—I had no clue where they were. Somewhere in the back of my mind, I knew I would never see them again.

Placing my jacket on my blanket, I rolled them and made a sling then started off. I walked the rest of the day. I could not believe I smelled smoke and could not see where it was coming from. I left the open range, happy to be out of the open. The range give way to a forest of thick trees and underbrush; going was not so easy.

I walked on for a while until darkness came with the feel of the chilly wind. I made a small fire. What I needed was water or something to drink. Making a bed of a few limbs, I spread my blanket over them, lying still because I was tired.

My thoughts carried me back to the crew. Somewhere in the late night, I fell asleep.

In the night, something woke me. I laid motionless, wrapped in my blanket, wondering what woke me—what did I hear? I had no weapon to defend myself if it was an animal or a human bandit. I never moved; I took short breaths. A voice said, "Rise, Paxton." I sat up and looked around; I saw nothing. What did I hear? Looking to the back of my rude camp, appearing from behind a tree was Hannah.

I said, "Well, Hannah, I was wondering when you were going to show up."

Hannah said in a reply, "I must keep you guessing, Paxton. You are on the right path. Keep walking; you will find a village. It is not time for you to meet the girls yet. Our timekeepers said to tell you to go to the village; this village is where the girls shop. You will see them, yet it is not time to meet. I will tell you this: your crew made it to Earth Paxton; there is nothing I can do for them."

I asked, "Then why am I special, Hannah? My crew needs to be rescued as I do; they know nothing of Earth or the human's cultures—they have no idea how to survive here. Please, Hannah; take them home. I know you have the power to do just that—if you can come to me like this, you have the power."

Hannah said, "Paxton, I cannot interfere, you must understand. The only thing I will tell you is that they will be fine; they will prosper here on earth. They are five hundred miles away, according to Earth's measures. Paxton, go back to sleep; tomorrow you will find this village. Go to a place and ask for employment. Until I or someone comes again, Zin said to tell you to believe in yourself. One day when you least expect it, you will meet Mimi. Paxton, do not tell anyone you are from space." Opening my eyes, I realized I had that dream again; looking around I saw no one.

From the color of the sky, I knew dawn was approaching; the gray color of the morning filled the eastern horizon. In my thoughts as I sat on my makeshift bed, I would have loved a cup of tea. The sound from my stomach told me a bread cake would be nice, also. Taking my jacket off, I rolled it in my blanket and tied it with a string. I slung the roll across my shoulder and started my journey, walking in the direction Hannah said for me to go.

I was not sure the distance I had traveled. The earth's sun was warm as I crested a small ridge. Looking into the distance, I saw a small village nestled in the small, green valley. Walking down and across the field, I saw some type of transportation vehicles. I wondered what they were called. Why there were so many of them? I looked at my clothes; I had mud all over me from the journey. I was a sight to behold, as one would say. I knew I would not fit in; well, I do not belong here. In my home world, we were so far advanced than these humans. Thinking of the talk I had with

Bota, you would think in the time that had gone by, Earth would be more advanced than they are.

My thoughts returned to my crew as I walked on; maybe some of them will transfer some knowledge to them. Walking into the path of the village, I thought on the worlds I have seen. I have never seen such buildings as these. Believe me, as I walked on I got the strangest looks from everyone. I suppose I was something to see. Walking on the funny path for a while, I saw this strange building.

It never dawned on me that on this day, humans were so primitive. Surely, they had better ways to do things. In the window of this building was a handwritten sign—I thought about how Hannah knew this. The sign read, "help wanted, apply inside."

I entered the building from the path. I knew right away it was a market; there were fruits and vegetable everywhere; there were dry goods and other things. On a stand, there was hanging what appeared to be human clothes. Well, this I could use—this would give me the chance to appear human, instead of from space, the one thing Hannah told me not to tell anyone. I thought, what a great idea to have all of this in one place. The fruit and vegetables, I knew what they were. I was not only a captain, believe it or not, but as a child on Ticoru I played in the fields and orchards. The ones that worked in the fields and orchards my father employed, I was always learning from them. The only thing I did not understand was how they get the seeds here to grow; I thought they were only from my world.

Walking around inside, I saw this man I thought would be the proprietor, so I asked of the job. He looked at me in an unusual way and pointed another way. I looked around to check my surroundings as I moved closer.

I said, "Sir, I am called Paxton. I am inquiring about the sign in the window." The man looked at me with a smile on his face. Looking me up and down he said, "You must be from space?" Well, my heart kind of slowed. How did he know? I thought. "Why would you say that?" I asked.

The man smiled, "Well, you sure are not from Russia, not dressed like that. Do you have experience in the work I have?" I told him I could get by. Moving to another box and around the table he asked, "Where are you from, son?" I smiled and told him I was from a long way away. He said, "Yes, I am sure you are; however, you are not from Russia, so everyone has got to be from somewhere."

He told me to come back tomorrow. "Go home, rest, and come back tomorrow ready for work." I told him I have no home, that I have been traveling for a long while—my pocket stone is all I have; I found it in the forest one day. I showed it to him. Looking at the stone, his eyes exploded in size. "What did you say your name was again?" I told him.

"Well Paxton, may I hold the nugget?" I passed it to him. He said, "Paxton, I do not believe you found this in the forest."

I answered, "Well, sir, I did find it by a stream where I stayed one night. Now, sir, I told you my name—what may I call you?"

Replying, he said, "My name is Merkoff."

I asked, "Sir, could you tell me what it could be worth here?" "Enough," he replied. "I know someone that might buy this; he will give you as decent price, I will see to that. Paxton, from the way you look, you have no place to stay—come with me."

I picked up my roll and walked behind him, passing the man I asked first. There was something strange about the way he stared; I feel I will have trouble with him. Following Merkoff outside the building to a smaller one, Merkoff told me his son lived here long ago. "He left to join the Russian army; my son never came back." I must say, it was a wonderful place. It had all I would need until I meet these girls Hannah talked about. I was not sure where I was to meet them. Merkoff left me standing as he walked out the door. He told me we start at five o'clock tomorrow morning, that there would be trucks to unload and two trucks to load. I told him I would be there. I suppose I was fortunate to meet Merkoff. Well after all, Hannah did send me.

The place was small, yet I would survive. I found the place to bathe. I took a bath—believe me I needed one. In one corner, I found a place to cook. That was something at which I was not good. I was about to take my shirt off when someone knocked on the door. I was waiting on someone to say captain. Suddenly, it occurred to me I was not on my ship, thanks to Kalean. I was on Earth, and I do not belong here. I knew no one on Earth except Merkoff. I knew Hannah, yet she was not from here.

Opening the door, Merkoff stood with his hand out. In his hand, he held some funny-looking paper. I looked at what was in his hand.

I asked, "Merkoff, what is this and what do I do with it?" Merkoff smiled at me as he handed it over.

Merkoff said, "It is rubles, Paxton, it is how you will pay for what you need. You buy things and you pay with rubles." I was totally confused. I took the paper from Merkoff and started to close the door when I heard him say, "Man, you really are not from Russia." I had no clue. Merkoff told me I could pay him back when he sold my nugget. Closing the door, I watched him go back to his shop.

I put my dirty clothes back on, took the rubles and went to the Merkoff's store, where I purchased a pair of trousers and a shirt. I went back to the place I was to live until I passed the guy that never talked.

Walking through the yard, the sun shone warm on my skin. I suppose the season had come to Russia. I changed into my new clothes and sat at the table, thinking why Zin could not have come through his portal and do what needed to be done. I had so many questions and no one to ask them to.

I went back to the place, took another bath and put my new clothes on. I thought I would take a walk. I walked through the shop to the main path that I found was called a street. I was also told the motor units were called cars of some sort. Technology had come to this part of the world; everything was electric except the flying machines. The one with the propeller was called a helicopter. I was in a strange world; a world I did not belong—there was no way to get off this planet; all I could do was wait. This world was nothing compared to Ticoru or the Moon of Spores.

Walking about, I caught a smell of food cooking. I was not sure what it was; all I knew was I wanted it. I was hungry and the smell was intensifying. A young girl with a snarly looked walked to me.

She asked, "May I help you, sir?" I told her I was hungry, and she led the way to a table. I told her I was not from Russia and asked what would she suggest.

She replied, "A hamburger, fries, and a coke." The smell of this place was outstanding; I would like to come here again. The young girl brought me my food. I must say, it was so good or I was extremely hungry—yet it was both. In my life, I had never had anything so delightful; this I would have again.

The young girl came to my table and she told me to pay the bill. I gave her some of the rubles Merkoff give me. She smiled and said, "You sure, sir? That is quite a bit." I never said anything, just walked to the door. She asked me where I was from. I told her I was from a long way from here. Walking out the door, I told her I would see her again. Walking down the street, I had a feeling someone was watching me. I stopped several times to check things in the windows. In a shop next door to Merkoff's there it was—I saw a reflection in the window. I was right; someone was watching me. I never let on that I saw him.

Somewhere, a loud sound came from overhead. Looking up, I saw a craft fly by. I noticed the man looked up, too. I took a quick step into Merkoff's shop. Looking through the window, the man was walking down the street toward Merkoff's shop. A craft flew overhead as I stepped back into the street. The man stopped before the door. I spoke to him, "How fast do you think they can go?" The man looked shocked at what I said. In a heavy Russian accent he said, "What? What did you say?" I repeated myself by saying, "How fast can they fly?" He mumbled something as he walked away.

I went back inside the shop and through the back to my place. Walking in, I sat down and picked up a book. The sun was warm shining through the window; somewhere in my thoughts and the warmth of the sun, I feel asleep.

CHAPTER 13

TIMES COMES AND IT GOES; THERE IS NOTHING I know of that time waits on. Time is an uncertain thing, but a for certain thing. Time is like death—there is no telling when it will catch up to you, yet I assure you it will.

I was not sure how long I had been asleep. I do know it was very much daylight when I fell asleep, and now it was full dark. My room was completely dark. It was hard to see in it with the dirt over the window. It was just as hard to see out. I stood to go to bed when I saw the man that was following me standing outside the store. He was talking to the employee of Merkoff's; I knew I was going to have trouble with him. I had decided the first time I did, I would just kill the bastard; hide his ass in the brush somewhere. I couldn't have him following me. Yes, seeing this out through the dirt, I decided that is just what I would do. I would have Merkoff send me on a truck somewhere and I would have this man come along. Since I could not drive a truck, he could. Then, I would do what needed to be done. I could not drive a car; it is funny that I could pilot a ship thousands of miles per hour, yet I could not drive one of the earth's vehicles.

Until the day this transpired, I would need to be weary of the two. I will find what mystery there is here in this place called Vologda, Russia. I went over to my bed, took my clothes off, laid on the bed, and fell asleep.

It seemed I had just closed my eyes when the night came alive with a sound from overhead. Dressing, I ran outside. I could not see anything; I stepped outside when Merkoff yelled he was coming to get me.

I asked, "Merkoff, what was with the plane flying so low?"

Merkoff said, "Damn Russian air force do this all the time, Paxton. I guess I pissed them off again. They fly over my store to scare me." I did not know what to say; I told him, "Well, it worked on me. I thought a UFO had hit me."

Merkoff laughed out loud, "Paxton, what do you know of UFOs?" I told him I have seen several in my lifetime. Well, I did not lie—Merkoff told me the air force did this on the way to the coast on patrol. "Come, Paxton. We work now."

I will say one thing: this was work. It was not what a captain was used to. I worked hard, and I noticed Merkoff had a smile the whole time. I would stack the fruit while Merkoff would take it inside the store. He would carry the boxes to the guy I first met; I thought I would ask about him later.

From one truck unloading to loading another one, the work was fast. Merkoff said I was a great worker and that was enough to keep me going. Stopping for a moment, my thoughts went to my crew. I swear, if Zin comes for me, I will ask him to go for my crew or ask if it would even be possible. If not, I must forget about them. When I return home, I will need to tell all the families.

Merkoff wheeled around the corner of the truck, "Paxton, you ok? It appears you are troubled." I told him I was thinking of home. He told me again that I was a good worker. "I know you are not used to this, but you do good work."

Merkoff said we were going to take a break for breakfast. Well, I had no problem with that—I was so hungry.

Walking to the same café I had visited before, the same girl led us to a table. Merkoff ordered what he called an omelet; I told the girl I would have the same. We both had coffee; it was not my first-time drinking coffee. I did have it when I visited Boldlygo. It truly was good. The young girl that waited on me before stopped by and said hello. She said it was good to see me. I just smiled and nodded. I did ask her how long she had worked here. She told me she was going to school here when a damn freaky girl got her expelled. I swear to you, I wanted to kill her. I tell you, something about that bitch is not right. "I see you work with Merkoff. You will meet her; she goes there all the time with her aunt." I asked her name, and she replied by saying Nina. I never told her mine.

Merkoff said, "Paxton, if you are not here long, stay away from her. I tell you now: she is trouble." I could see what he was saying; she had the look—especially the hair; I have never seen a female with that color hair.

The week ended, then another. One day I was placing apples on a stand when two beautiful women came into the store; one was younger than the other. For some reason, I thought I knew them, though I have never met them. I watched them closely as they moved up and down the aisles. The older one saw me gazing. She smiled as she walked to me.

She asked, "You are knew here? I have never seen you before." I told her I had been working about three weeks.

She said, "Well, my niece and I come her often; maybe I will see you again." Without thinking, I said out loud: "I sure hope so." The younger one elbowed her, laughing. They both laughed as they made their way to the counter. I watched them as they left the store. She turned as she went out the door, smiling. I thought, Earth girls no different than other girls I have met. Like Mora—Mora was a beautiful woman. I was kind of getting attached to her, then all this shit happen with Kalean.

Merkoff walked over to the stand. Placing a box of apples down, he told me to come to his office. I crushed the boxes by placing a strap on them, then took off my apron as I made my way to the office.

I admit the brief time I have been here on Earth that I had grown fond of Merkoff. He did treat me differently than the other two males that were employed by him. The one I met the first time—well what could I say about him? I knew we would come to blows soon. Merkoff and I had become friends. Of course, I did think of my crew often.

Entering the office, Merkoff pointed to a chair. In Merkoff's heavy Russian accent he said, "My friend, when you come to me about work, you gave me a nugget of gold." To tell you the truth, I had almost forgotten about it.

Merkoff said, "I did as I said I would do. I sold the nugget for two hundred fifty thousand rubles; this will last you a long while, Paxton." Merkoff handed me an envelope. Opening it up, I saw it was stuffed with Russian money. I took some of the rubles and gave them to him.

Merkoff said, "Paxton, I do not need your money; I would like to know where you got it. My friend said to me no gold could be found on Earth as pure as this gold nugget. He told me there is no gold in Russia or anywhere that could compare." I did not know what to say, so I let it pass. Well, at least I hope it did.

I said, "Merkoff, at least let me buy you dinner at the café." Merkoff agreed. I went to my place to change clothes while Merkoff closed the store. Walking to the café, I saw the employee of Merkoff's talking to another man pointing my way, and many thoughts ran through my mind. I thought I was going to kill this man if he gave me a problem. I believe that time will come, sooner than later.

Entering the cafe, Nina was the first person I saw, and believe me she is not the one I was looking for. Before I left my place, the two girls that were in the store the other day went in the café. Nina told me Merkoff was sitting in the back, next to the two bitches. Believe me, I did not understand what the human expression was, so I went on to the table.

As I sat down, I said: "Look, things here in Russia are different from where I am from. So, I must ask—why did Nina call them a bitch as I pointed to the girls?" Well, I could see the anger building inside the younger ones eyes; I have always been able to see this. I get that from my mother.

Merkoff said, "Paxton, that it not a nice thing to say about a woman here." I looked at the girls, and I told them I meant no disrespect. The older one told me it was ok, you did not know. The girls stood, left the table, and walked to the street. Walking through the door, she turned to look at me, giving me a huge smile. Nina came from the back carrying a large tray when she stumbled and fell. The young girl laughed as she followed the other one to the street. I told Merkoff I had no idea what I was saying; I was just repeating what I had heard.

The thing I have learned is it does not matter what world you are from—all women are the same. They sometimes will lead you with that same smile I received from the lady.

The time I have been here on Earth was the same as on any planet—time comes and goes; it waits on nothing, just as it does on Earth. From time to time, I thought of my crew. I wondered if they were well. I wondered why Hannah had not come to me. Kalean's ship was destroyed; I did that with my ship diving into him—besides, Kalean and his crew could not survive on Earth. If—and I do mean if—he made it out, someone would kill him. Destroying him was the right thing to do. When you rid yourself of one problem, another one surely will appear.

Sitting out back of the store drinking a cold drink, the summer heat was on as Merkoff says. I was enjoying my cold drink when two Russian soldiers approached me. I always enjoyed my orange drink, but they were interrupted me. They started asking me all kind of questions like, "Who are you? Where are you from? Do I live here?" I stood as Merkoff came from the back. "Paxton, come help me close."

One said, "This man is going nowhere."

I said, "Excuse me, this is my employer; I must help him." I left them standing as I walked into the store. I could see through the store to the street; the huge window concealed nothing. I saw the man that worked with Merkoff standing on the curb talking to someone. I asked Merkoff who he was and Merkoff told me he was Russian police.

Watching through the window I said, "Merkoff, why would the Russian police be interested in me?"

Merkoff replied, "They may not be so interested in you, but where you are from. Paxton, the Russian police have asked about you; it would appear you have raised suspicion. The police have no record of you."

"Merkoff, it makes no sense. What difference does it make where I am from?"

Merkoff said, "Paxton let me tell you this." Merkoff started his story as he pointed to the office. Walking through the fruit to his office, Merkoff pointed to a chair; there were papers all over the desk and chairs.

And the floor. Merkoff sat behind his desk then started his story. "A few weeks ago, a ship of some kind was seen over Russia. There was a scare in the Russian government."

I said, "What does that have to do with me?"

Merkoff said, "Do you see, Paxton, you showed up at the time of the explosion. The Russian police are watching you and others. Nina, the girl at the café, she was sent to a school to spy. She did not fit in, so she was expelled. I have a cousin; his daughter goes there and she tells her father, then he tells me things. Paxton, I believe him, that is why I tell you to stay away from that Nina girl. Paxton, if you want a girlfriend, go for Sophia—you know her; she is the one with the beautiful young girl."

Smiling I said, "Yes, Merkoff; I do know what you mean. Look, Merkoff, I have grown fond of you, but someday I will leave. I do not know when, but I think soon. Maybe I will take you with me. Someday soon, someone will come for me. I do not want to attach myself to anything. Merkoff, have you lived here in Russia your whole life?"

Merkoff said, "Paxton, I am fifty years old; I have lived in Russian and here in Vologda my whole life. I will tell you this: here in this village, I have seen so much. The ship that was seen, it was not my first time hearing about a flying ship. I am telling you, just be careful." I started out the door then turned around. "Merkoff," I said, "maybe you should come with me." Merkoff let out a huge laugh. "Who would I leave my store to?" I told him that would be up to him. "I know one thing if you do. Merkoff, you will never come back. That is all I can say." Merkoff give out another huge laugh, making a jester with his hand to leave. Walking on through the door, I let out a laugh and said, "Merkoff, I am not joking."

CHAPTER 14

I PLACED MY HAND TO MY FACE AS TO CUP MY FACE. I started to think about the conversation Paxton and I had. Why did he say that the way he did? What did he mean? I knew Paxton was different the moment I saw him. In my life, I have heard so many stories of being from space. I once had family that said the same. One day, some of them disappeared and I never heard from them again. I cannot believe he is from, well, you know…space.

The only thing I know other than what I have read is that space is out there. I cannot say I have ever met someone from space. Standing from my desk, I walked to the window, and I saw the Russian police. Why have they started hanging around my store? This was bad for my business.

I noticed Russian police never come by my place until Paxton came here. Russian police never say much, they just act. One week after Paxton shows up, they start hanging around. Standing across the street, in the café, and now in back. I see Anton talking to them sometimes. I remember when he worked for me; it was only a short while. He left about the same time Russia police went to the school. I do remember he would talk to the girls, Sophia, and her niece. She is so good of a person.

My thoughts went to Paxton. I mean, who really appears all muddy and out of the woods and plains? I do believe there is more to Paxton than I first believed. I thought he was a nice young man who just lost his way—well, that was until he handed me the gold nugget. My friend, the nugget was not from this world. Well, where was it from? How did Paxton get his hands on the nugget? Was he part of the explosion? As I have said, there is more to Paxton than I believe. Paxton told me he might take me with him; he said someone was coming for him. How would they come here? So many questions with no answers.

If he is from space, why did he come to Russia? Oh my, now he has me believing he is from space. How bizarre is that?

I left my office to lock the door. A Russia policeman was standing in the doorway.

I asked, "Sir, may I help you?" He just looked at me for what seemed like minutes.

He said, "Yes, you may. The young man you have employed here, how long have you known him? Does he plan on staying here and for how long."

Replying, I said, "Not long. I do not know, I have no clue, and I do not know." The policeman looked at me.

"What do you mean? Are you being stupid?" I told him I answered all his questions. "Sir, it will be up to you to unravel it. Sir, I am not being stupid. I have a successful business; I did not get here by being stupid. Now sir, if you will excuse me, it has been a long day; I would like to go home."

He said, "I am Yuri, Russian police, you do not talk to me like that." I told him I knew who he was. "Sir, I do not care. I have been here for a long time. I never have had trouble with the Russian police. In the future, if you need fruits and vegetables, come see me. In the meantime, stay away from my store and my employees. Now sir, I must insist: please leave." He told me he would be back. I told him I open at five in the morning and close at six in the evening. "You want fine fruits and vegetables, come here." I locked the door as he entered the street.

I was thinking of Paxton when the police entered the street. What was going on here? Why was they so inserted in him? I wondered—was he, or could he be, from space? Walking to the back of the store, I saw Paxton leave the building to the alley. I knew where he was going. I closed the back door and walked to the café. I noticed Anton was on the far side of the street. He never looked up as he was talking to the Russian police. Tomorrow, I will have a chat with him. I will see if Anton can speak on this without revealing too much.

I must admit when he worked for me before, something was off about him, and I still believed this. Walking through the door, Paxton saw me enter the door. He waved to me, motioning to come to his table. Walking over to him and sitting down I said, "Paxton, the mystery man. Paxton, there are people wanting to know about you and where you are from." Paxton told me there was no mystery about him; he said this with a wink of the eye.

Inside the café, there were nothing going on since it was a Wednesday. I did ask about his friend, Nina. Paxton told me he had not seen her when our waitress approached the table and asked if we were ready to order. I was about to give her my order when six Russian police came through the door. Paxton and I looked at each other as they walked to the table. I picked the one out I thought was in charge, and asked, "Sir, may I help you?" The officer said, "You are Merkoff?" I told him I was. "You are to come with me, and your friend, also."

I said, "Yes of course, but could we eat first?" He told us that this will not take long. Standing, we started to walk to the door when one of the assholes took a swing at Paxton. I am not sure how Paxton knew the swing was coming, but he ducked as the police tried to recover. The police swung so hard he lost his balance, falling to the floor. I will tell you if he had connected, Paxton would have been in trouble. Paxton sat back down and the police reached for him. Paxton said, "You really do not want to touch me."

They are times when people just do not listen. I consider myself old compared to Paxton; I said nothing. I watched and observed. It was amazing to see this—I am not sure where he took his training; to watch him in action was awesome. He moved better than a platoon of Russian commando. The end result was six Russian police on the floor, wondering what the hell just happened. Paxton stooped over, telling the police, "You should have listened to me. I was coming with you. Do not ever touch me."

Here in Russia, there is a saying: you have pissed me off. I never moved from my chair. There were two more police that came running in, and it was Yuri. In his Russian accent he yelled, "You are coming with me." Paxton replied, "I am not going anywhere with you." Yuri looked around at his men lying on the floor: "You do not hit Russian police."

Paxton stood and pointed his finger at Yuri. "I was coming peacefully; your man swung at me for no reason. He asked; I gave. Now, if you want me to come along, go to your magistrate and retrieve a warrant." Paxton looked at me, "Is that what it is called, Merkoff?"

"It is, Paxton." I said.

Yuri screamed, "You will pay for this."

Paxton told me he would go to the magistrate and find out what was going on. Walking out the door, Paxton told the girl he would be back to pay the damage. She said, "Do not worry about it; there has never been this much excitement since I have owned the place." Paxton started to leave and I told him I was coming along; I told him I knew the magistrate very well.

Leaving the café for my vehicle, I asked Paxton where he trained to fight. He replied, "I held a prominent position in the air force; it was expected of me." I drove to the village of Vologda. The magistrate's office was next to the police. Parking next to the building, we walked inside together. Yuri was standing inside and he was telling his story when he saw us walk in. He yelled, "That is him, arrest him." The magistrate walked out of his office to see the problem. The magistrate said, "For what reason do we arrest him?"

Yuri screamed, "He beat several of my officers. I want him arrested." The magistrate looked at Paxton, then to me, and said: "Merkoff, what is happening here? Merkoff bring your friend into my office. Yuri, you come along, too."

Inside the office, the magistrate took his seat. He said, "Yuri, I will have no interruption, you understand?" Looking at Yuri then to me, he said, "Tell me, Merkoff, in your own words."

I said, "This man," pointing at Paxton, "he is an employee of mine. He comes into the village wandering around asking for job. I gave him job. Magistrate, I am sure you know there has been several complaints about Yuri." "Yes Merkoff, I am aware of the complaints." The magistrate asked, "Are you still harassing the school, Yuri?" Looking at me, Yuri said nothing. "Magistrate, I am not sure why Yuri is doing what he is doing. He has officers standing outside of my business. Sir, as you know, this is bad for my business."

Yuri jumped up, "It is my belief that he is from space and causes a threat to Mother Russia. This man showed up after the explosion and sighting of a UFO—what am I to believe? The girl at school—I believe she is, too. Her aunt was also believed to be from space."

Slapping the top of his desk, the magistrate stood. "Yuri, leave these people alone. From space, my ass. Now get the hell out of my office. Merkoff, you and your friend are free to go."

Yuri said, "What about the assault on my officers?" "Get out, Yuri, get out!" He told him. I did not say much on the way back to the store; I told Paxton as we pulled up, "Son, one day we are going to have a long talk. Paxton, it is not that far off. Soon, the women holiday comes, then we talk. Now go to bed; it is getting late. Five a.m. comes early, Paxton."

Paxton opened the door to exit the car, when two girls came from the street. Sophia and Mimi walked to my side. Talking in Russian, Sophia walked over to Paxton.

Sophia said to Paxton, "I asked Merkoff if you could come to our home this weekend for dinner. He said you worked until noon on Saturday." I smiled and as she turned to walk away, she looked back.

Paxton asked, "Are you always this forward?" Sophia told him only when I see something I want. Sophia walked to the car. Her niece said, "Well Sophia, he is very handsome, I will say that."

The week was progressing great; nothing much happened. I saw nothing of the Russian police from the time at the magistrate office until Friday. Then Saturday morning, it started again. They must have heard of Paxton going to the home of Sophia. Watching through the window, I saw two of them standing across the street. Paxton came to me, and he told me he was taking a walk to the park. "There is a big fountain there; I like to sit and listen to the water."

Paxton walked to the park as planned, taking a drink with him. I noticed the police left as he walked out the door. Neither one approached him. Sitting on the bench, Paxton told me later that Nina girl showed up. He said he went there to think and she appeared from behind a big tree; it was like she knew he was going to be there. "Nina came closer and I thought oh no. I saw no one else. She walked straight to me. I can say one thing about her: this girl could really talk. As you said, the bullshit was heavy. I had no clue something else was about to happen. I looked over Nina's shoulder, and I saw Sophia's niece walking toward me. Coming closer she spotted Nina, and you could see the hate in Mimi's eyes. She hated Nina with a passion.

"Nina turned as Mimi spoke. Nina said, 'damn, freak, cannot go anywhere without you. You messed up my life, you little freaking bitch.'

"I said, 'Wait, what is going on here?'

"Nina said, 'This is the freak from school; this is the bitch I told you about. You know, the one in the diner.'

"I said, 'Her name is Mimi; she is not a freak, Nina.' Nina started to leave when Mimi said, 'You remember the ass kicking I gave you at school? Would you like to have a repeat?' Nina never said a word, but she ran away fast. Mimi was walking away and I said to her, 'I do not think you are a freak, or that word she called you again. I think you are a nice girl, and your aunt, too.' Mimi said, 'I will talk to you when you come to our house for dinner, handsome.' Well, I was all that.

"Turning away, her eyes watered. 'Paxton, I am not a freak; my aunt Sophia said I was different.' Sophia drove up to Mimi, and she was drying her eyes as I told her what had happened.

"Sophia asked, 'Why are you here?' I told her I was sitting by the fountain when this Nina girl came up. We started to talk, then Mimi showed up. One thing led to another.

"Sophia said, 'Look, there might be something that will scare you about us; you can feel free to cancel dinner if you like. I would not say a thing.'

"I said, 'Well, if you do not want to cook.' Sophia said, 'Oh no, it is something else.'

"Sophia said, 'Well, ok, then. Until tomorrow.' I told her I had a few things about me, too. 'Look, I am sure we will find common ground. We can learn as we go; I work until noon.'

"Sophia said, 'Good, Mimi and I close the school about that time. We will come by and pick you up. We live about a thirty-minute drive from here. There is so much to talk about.' I agreed.

"Walking back to the store, I had a feeling there was more to this than I see. In my thoughts, this girl Mimi would kill Nina the first chance she gets or injure her in some horrible way. Like Kalean, he got what he deserved; so will Nina. Just as I would the man Anton in the store, if he causes me hardship while I am here. Anton never said anything, yet was always hanging around the Russian police."

I only knew one day I would leave; I am not sure what Hannah meant. She did say I would meet the girls and maybe this is what she was talking about. I am sure time will tell.

Saturday morning came as any other did. I poured a cup of coffee and walked to the window. I took a drink, seeing someone. "Damnit," I said, "Russian police." Walking to the door I yelled, "Can I help you?" He started to run and fell over a crate, falling face in the dirt. I walked over, looked down, and said: "You know a person can get hurt or even killed snooping around."

He replied, "I am Russian police; you do not scare me." I told him I was not trying to scare him; I told him I was stating a fact. I offered my hand. He took hold as I pulled him to a standing position. I said, "Now, why were you here? I know you do not steal, so why were you here?" Merkoff came from the store. "Paxton, I was coming to get you. Who is this, Paxton?"

I said, "Merkoff, we have certified Russian police here."

Merkoff said in his heavy accent, "Asshole, why are you snooping in my store—leave now, asshole." I could not help

from laughing out loud. Merkoff had a smile on his face
as we went to my place for coffee. "Damn Russian police;
damn asshole." Inside, Merkoff sat the table as I poured a
cup for him. He said, "You know, Paxton, in two days I have
had more fun than my in my whole life. Paxton, remember
I told you one day we need to talk; maybe today is that day."

I said, "Well, Merkoff, you need to open the store." I
poured another cup. I said, "Merkoff, what is on your mind."

Merkoff said, "First thing, Paxton, where you are from?
I do need to know this." Setting my cup down, I reached
for a bag of what is called cake pops; I find they go good
with coffee. "Merkoff, you would not believe me, besides a
friend that I have not heard from in a while told me not to
say where I was from."

Merkoff said, "You can tell me; I will not say a word."

I said, "When I return this weekend, Merkoff, I will have
that talk you wish for. I do plan to have a good weekend.
Now Merkoff, let us go open the store."

Unlocking the back door, turning on the light, and walking to the front of the store, Paxton was on the street. I knew
what he was looking for—the same thing I was looking for,
the Russian police. It was around six o'clock; the village was
alive. Since the day Paxton had arrived, today would be the
first time he would be away from my supervision. I do hope
he has a good day.

Outside, the morning air was cool. The birds were flying close to the ground, singing their songs. You could tell

spring was in the air; spring flowers had started to shoot up. Today was going to be a good day, I thought.

Looking across the street, there is an old building with a clock made into the wall that read ten o'clock. Paxton had gone back to the back to unload a truck that had come in during the night. A very loud boom came as seven Russian planes flew over. I ran to the back. Here in the village, the planes woke up the people. The Russian air force had started their patrol. Just out of curiosity, I looked up, then said to myself: now he has gotten me to doing it, looking for something that is not there.

I believe Paxton is from space—think about it: this man shows up here in Russia at the time a ship was seen. A man from the plains, all muddy and with no money. Well, everyone has got to be from somewhere. I do believe out there, somewhere in space, is where he is from. I could not be sure of this, but I feel he will tell me when the time is right. I mean, he did tell me he would take me with him when he leaves. Maybe I will tell someone I might leave. I know several people, yet I was not sure who to leave it with if I did go. I mean, if I died, what then? This I must think on.

I was taking fruit from a box and placing it on a stand when a voice said hello. I turned to see a young man standing in front of the store. Walking toward him, I could see he was well dressed. I do not believe I have ever seen him before.

I asked, "May I help you, sir?" He replied in a Russian accent, "I am supposed to meet two young ladies here today.

They will be taking an employee of yours to their home for the weekend. I do believe his name is Paxton." I told the young man they have not arrived, yet I knew them. I suppose they are still at school. The young man introduced himself as Ivan. I told him Paxton worked until noon. He ask if he could wait. I told him to sit on a box or he could wait in my office. He told me the bench would be fine. In my mind, he was a well-educated man. Him and I spoke from time to time until the damn Russian police entered the building. The first thing he asked was where was Paxton? I said, "What now? What do you want with him? You need to leave him alone." This was different police, and he was sure of himself—sure to the point that I did not like him; I saw this right away. I told him Paxton was out back unloading a truck; he started to walk to the back.

I said, "Leave him alone, I damn well mean it."

Replying, he smiled at me, "You do not talk to the Russian police like that. I will make things hard for you, do you understand me?" Little did I know what was about to happen. In fact, Paxton could fight—I never knew he could do what he did. Approaching Paxton, I saw his arm go up and a crate flew across the yard, hitting the police and knocking him to the ground. Paxton walked over, looking down at the man. Paxton said, "Employees only in the back." The man tried to stand; he was staggering, as he was intoxicated. His nose was bleeding and he also had a cut over his eye. I laughed; good enough for him, he got what he deserved. Paxton came inside and told me what had happened. I told him employees only in back. The police was pissed; he said as he started to leave that he would be back. I told him I open at five, close at six. "That is Monday through Saturday; come anytime."

The girls showed up and the young man that was waiting joined them. Paxton went to his place, changed into fresh clothes, and was gone. I gave a big sigh of relief.

·

CHAPTER 15

I LEFT MERKOFF'S STORE AND MIMI TOLD ME TO ride in the front. I had no clue where we were going, but I did enjoy riding in an Earth vehicle. I tell you it was far different than the way we moved around on Ticoru; this was different from other planets I had been on. Boldlygo, for instance, they had no cars. I do believe Aries moved around from village to the palace in what is called a scruple, a small craft that carries several people.

Sophia told me as we moved along that her and Mimi lived in Moscow. She introduced Ivan, since I had no clue who he was. She said Ivan had lived with Tasha since he was eight; Sophia said Ivan was family. She said, "I do think of him as my brother." I replied to her, "I have no brother or sister." I took in the countryside as Sophia drove. Mimi never said much, and when she did, her words would be in Russian. Sophia would laugh—no doubt it was about me.

In my thoughts, for some reason, I knew they were the girls Hannah told me about; funny how things work out. Sophia said something in Russian. Ivan looked at me, then to Sophia, then back to me.

Ivan asked, "Paxton, do you eat meat? And where are you from?" I was not sure how to answer him, so I said, "Sometimes, not too often." He said something to Sophia. She pulled into a market. Looking into the rearview, she smiled as her and Mimi exited the vehicle and walked inside, picking at each other. I really do not understand Earth people.

Ivan asked, "Paxton how long have you been here in Russia?" I told him I had not been here long, about two months. "I come from a place...well it is a long way from here. The only way to go to my home is by ship." Ivan looked at me with that look.

Ivan said, "You cannot go there by plane?" I told him no, only by ship.

Ivan said, "So you live on an island?" I did not answer, as Mimi was running towards the car. Mimi ran to my side of the car. Mimi said, "Paxton, come help Sophia—there is a man giving her a tough time."

I flew from the car running inside the market, a Russian policeman was trying to take her arm.

I yelled at him, "You! Stop, now!"

Looking at me, he said: "You do not talk to me like that; I am Russian police." I eased my way over to him. "Well, would you rather me kick your ass as I did your comrade?" I laughed out loud.

Replying, he said, "Do not be absurd; you cannot fight me, I am Russian"—that is all he said, because I kicked his ass and left him on the floor. Sophia paid the man and I took her arm, leaving the store. The Russian policeman was still lying on the floor.

Sophia was the color of the clouds when we reached the car. She told Mimi and Ivan what happened. Mimi reached over the seat, saying, "You are a good man, Paxton."

I said, "Mimi, I do not think much of a man that mistreats women. That would never happen where I am from." Sophia said, "We are almost there." Sophia said something in Russian; Ivan told me when we arrived, he would show me around. "Sophia and Mimi will cook. We will eat good and talk about all kinds of thing. You wait; you will see." I did not say much of anything; I mostly listen and smiled.

Pulling into the driveway; I will say one thing: it was a big house. Walking up the steps and going inside, I saw that there were windows everywhere. Looking around, there was a big chair sitting by a huge window. Ivan told me Tasha would sit there all day; sometimes into the night. "She would meditate; sometimes I could hear her talking to people." Looking at Ivan, I said, "Then she was not well, you know."

I answered, "No, I do not know; tell me."

Replying, I said, "Ivan, you said you could hear her talking to people—do you not find that a little strange?"

Ivan said, "I never thought about it. Tasha had this power about her; she talked to several people. I never did hear anyone answer, but she would talk to Zin, Leah, and Mayrra. I do not know who they are; I suppose they are either dead or gone." Well, now he had my attention.

Ivan said, "They live somewhere else. They do not live in Russia, but I have never asked where." Ivan showed me the big house. There were rooms everywhere. Ivan told me that Tasha passed away several months ago. "You know, Paxton, just about the time you came to Russia."

I said, "I had nothing to do with that." Mimi laughed out loud; she was behind me.

Mimi said, "Paxton, you say the funniest things. Aunt Tasha died from old age; Tasha was incredibly old. Aunt Tasha was a beautiful person; you would have loved her and the stories she could tell." I did not say a word about me being from space, but I think they already knew. I did ask Mimi if she ever heard Tasha talk to people.

Mimi said, "When Tasha would meditate, she talked to several people." I said, "You did not find that strange? Or you believed she was talking to someone?"

Mimi said, "Tasha had an extraordinarily strong mind. I do believe she could go anywhere. I believe she could go to Boldlygo." I almost choked—I started coughing and gasping for breath.

Mimi asked, "You alright, Paxton?" My face had turned red from coughing, and through a course voice I said, "Yes, I am fine." Sophia walked into the room and asked if I liked the house. I told her it was huge; Sophia told me when they leave, the house belongs to Ivan.

I asked, "You are leaving? Where are you going?" Sophia said she was not sure, but it would be soon. "I cannot say for certain; just soon, Paxton." I knew in that moment these were the two girls Hannah was talking about. Now I was anxious to find out, but I waited until the time was right to ask. Mimi saying Boldlygo was enough, yet it did not seem to register to them. I waited for a reaction; I saw none. I wondered if they knew what was happening. It makes one wonder how they knew that word. Sophia told us it was time to eat. Ivan and I went to the washroom to wash up. Walking into the dining area, I stopped in the doorway. The smell was awesome. On the table there was some kind of meat and what I took to be vegetables. Well, let me say, they were green, anyway. I admit the cafe where I have eaten most of my meals was good, but nothing as good as this.

I took several spoons of each thing on the table; I also took a generous portion of the meat. We were enjoying a friendly conversation and eating, and I had to ask. "Mimi, what was that word you said earlier? What did it mean?"

Mimi said, "What word, Paxton? I am not sure the word?"

I said, "It was a word I have never heard before, like Boldlygo or something. What does that mean?"

Mimi explained, "Well, Paxton," looking at Sophia "you see, an exceedingly long time ago, a group of beings came to Earth. I suppose as our family history tells us, they were from Boldlygo. It is a word I suppose that has been passed through time. Sometimes we still use it; it is a planet somewhere in a universe. I am not sure where."

I was curious, so I listened to the talk. Ivan said, "Tasha has told me of this since I was a small child. That alone was a long time ago. I sat many nights listening to her talk about the king and queen." I stood as each looked at me, and I said, "Omega and Kira are not the king and queen of Boldlygo, it is Zin and Tressa." The girl stood and ran to me. In the kitchen from the far wall, a light appeared; the light grew as big as the wall. Tressa, Zin, Leah, Shila, Fina and Hannah stepped trough. Ivan fell to the floor, and Mimi and Sophia were the color of the clouds. As the light disappeared, I said to Zin: "Good to see you, my king. Zin, it took you long enough." Hannah spoke, "It is good to see all of you. Paxton, the time is right."

I said, "I suppose, but not for my crew." Sophia and Mimi looked at me. "What crew?" they said at the same time. I told them I was on a ship that got destroyed in space. "My crew and I escaped in pods. We were separated." Zin looked at the table of food.

Zin said, "If you are coming to our world, there will be no eating of meat at any time."

Leah said, "I am Leah, I am the mother of Zin. I have lived on Boldlygo for over four hundred years. Believe me, you will not miss it. The council has observed you from afar. We will give you one week to determine if you wish to come—it will be a one-way trip. Once we have gone, the chance to return will not happen. Mimi, since you are the last member of our Earth family, when you come home, there will be no reason to return. Let these humans do what they please. Today is Saturday; in one week we will come again. When we return, you will let us know if you wish to leave, if you wish to go to Boldlygo or Galaxo." I said, "I am ready now."

Shila said, "Paxton, Zin knows you wish to bring your employer. I do not think he believes you. You must find out. Tell him it will be as Zin said, it is a one-way trip. We know Mimi is the last blood; we thought Mayrra was. This Saturday you are to meet here, let us say three o'clock—be here and be ready; we will not stay long. Paxton, I know you are ready, yet you must stay here to protect them." I introduced Ivan to Zin. "Ivan will take over this place and all Tasha's belonging. Tasha has raised him since he was a child." Zin said, "I know of him, he does have family blood. His DNA is not strong enough to carry our family ties."

Leah spoke, "Paxton, remember I was born here in Russia; I know how the Russian police and army can be. Long ago, my husband came to Earth looking for Mea, and he found me. We did not know at the time we were sisters. Mea and I were to be executed by the Russian army, and Dorn saved us." The wall behind them opened as the light grew brighter. The wall opened and the girls could see the beauty of the planet. Tears fell down their faces.

Mimi said, "Oh my look! It is like heaven in space." The portal closed and they were gone. I reached down, took Sophia's hand, and asked: "Well, what do you think?" Sophia was still in shock; she could not speak she only nodded her head.

I said, "Well, now we know. We no longer need to hide it from each other. I will talk to Merkoff; I think he is afraid. Nonetheless, I will ask him; he is a good man. If he does not wish to come along, I will be here. Zin said to be here next Saturday."

Sophia said, "Hannah told us about you. I am happy it was you. Paxton, I am not sure I want to go. If I go, where do I go: Galaxo, or Boldlygo?"

I said, "Sophia, Zin will open the portal that will take me to my home world. If you wish, you could come to my world. I have never had a mate or a long relation with any female. In the past few weeks, I have had a strong feeling when you are close. I have never spoken of my world be- cause Hannah told me not to." Sophia poured a cup of tea as Ivan took a seat across from me.

Mimi said, "Paxton, why don't you tell us something about you? There has got to be more than what we have seen."

I said, "Well, I was captain of my ship. This ship belonged to my mother and father, just one of many in a fleet." Mimi's eyes got big; her nostrils flared as she seemed excited. "Look, you may find this hard to believe, but not only was I the captain, I am also a prince of my world. My mother and father are the queen and king of Ticoru. It is my world: I will take you there if you wish to go."

Ivan asked, "How is it you know the people of Boldlygo." I told them the story; I told them about the travel from the Moon of Spores because of Kalean. I filled them in on my travels to Earth and the many planets I stopped in, and the days I spent on Mars. "I wish you could see this from a ship. I cannot show them to you, because my ship was destroyed. Traveling through Zin's portal, you cannot see this." I did not leave anything out—I told them about my crew that I must leave here on earth. I said this would be an extremely awkward thing to do, to leave them here.

Mimi said, "Why can't you take them with you?" I told her I had no clue where they are. "You see, when they went for the pods, I stayed behind to destroy Kalean's ship. I have no idea where they landed. When the ship went down, it crashed. I ran for my pod and they were already gone; my coordinates were knocked off line when I entered Earth's atmosphere—so, I have no clue where or how to contact them. I feel some of them died; Hannah told me it was the way it must be. Mimi, it is no difference than you leaving here and leaving your friends."

Mimi said, "What friends? Only Ivan; Sophia is coming with me, or I will kick her ass." We had a good laugh. Mimi said, "The only thing I would really miss is knowing I did not get to kick Nina's ass. Oh, how I wanted to do that."

I laughed out loud. I said, "Mimi, this is Saturday afternoon; you could still get the chance. I would not stop you."

Sophia said, "Oh, hell, Paxton! Do not encourage her." We all laughed hard.

Ivan said, "That is why you would need a ship to go home; I was thinking a boat." Time slipped away as the night conversation went on.

I was yawning as the time was getting late. Sophia told me I could take Ivan's room, since he had moved into Tasha's room. I told them I did not know I was staying the night, but that I like that.

Mimi said, "Oh yes, we talked about this. I said maybe you and Sophia—" Sophia yelled at her, "That is enough!" I just laughed. I must say it was a hard laugh for the four of us. Looking at Mimi, she was laid out on the floor and was kicking her legs. I do not think I have ever seen someone laugh so hard. Sophia's face turned red and I knew what was going on. Sophia showed me to the room, and said, "I will see you in the morning, sir Paxton."

I said, "What is with the sir?"

Sophia replied, "Well, you said you were a prince."

I said, "Go to bed; I will see you in the morning." Closing the door, I turned on the light—it was a nice room. I went to the bed and pushed on it: nice and firm. I took off my clothes, slid under the covers, and ten minutes later I did not know I was alive. I do not believe I have ever slept so soundly.

There was a sound that brought me awake; it was a sound coming from the living room. I put on my clothes and opened the door; I could see daylight was here. I heard Sophia scream, I was leaving the room in a hard run just as Mimi came from her room. Ivan hit the stairs in a run. Looking in the living room, Sophia was on the floor. I was pissed: a Russian police officer stood over her. I reached for his shoulder to smack the hell out of him when he went flying into the wall. I was impressed; hell, I thought I did that, but it was not me—it was Mimi. I walked to him as he tried to rise. I picked Sophia up and took her to the sofa.

I asked, "You want to tell me what happened?" She told me Yuri came to the door,. "He wanted to know where you were. He demanded I tell him or he would do to me what he did to Merkoff. He said Merkoff was being held by two of his men."

He said they were in the place where you stay and that two others were there, also. I looked at Yuri lying on the floor. Ivan said he was knocked out.

I looked at Mimi, "Tell me how you threw his ass the way you did." Mimi started to say, but then Sophia interrupted. "She has powers of some kind. I do, too, Paxton. I am not as strong as her. Tasha would tell us of the females had powers if they had the gene. Only Zin was the strongest; Tasha said some men had powers, but none were as strong as Zin. Tasha said it was the way Maoke wanted it. Maoke passed this down through the DNA process, in what was called the DNA transfer in those days."

I looked at Mimi, "You want to take a ride with me?"

Mimi asked, "Can you drive, Paxton?"

I said "No." Sophia smiled at me as she said, "Got to take you back, anyway; I cannot believe you can fly a damn spaceship but you cannot drive a small car." I told her there was nothing in space to hit. I told Ivan to help me with Yuri. We put him in the trunk of Sophia's car then ran back to the house to dress. Leaving the house, Sophia asked, "Can Yuri breathe in the trunk?"

Mimi said, "It really does not matter, Sophia; he is going to die anyway. If we let him live, he will never leave Ivan alone, you know that." "I can do it; I will have no problem with it—besides Sophia, I am on a roll. Nina is next; I will fix that bitch for all the mean shit she has done to me and the other girls at the school. I may not kill her, but I will make her wish she were dead, I assure you of this."

Sophia said as she looked at Mimi, "Little girl, you need to control yourself." Replying, Mimi told her she was in control. Hell, I knew what that meant—Mimi told us they have messed with the wrong alien.

I said, "Wrong alien Mimi, really?" "Damn right, Paxton," Mimi said.

Sophia's eye had started to swell. I asked her if she was alright. She told me she was fine. Ivan was not saying much, and I found this to be exciting. I thought about Merkoff and wondered if he was hurt. Leah told us about them back when she was here and they have not changed—the Russian police thought they were superior in every way; you practically had to kneel to them. I do not believe in hitting a woman; I do not care what they have done. I told Mimi I had kicked two of the Russian police and I would do it again if I had to.

Mimi snickered, "Yeah Paxton, this time you got me." Sophia was enjoying this more than she was letting on; you could see a faint smile sometimes from the corner of her mouth. Ivan was still not saying much.

Sophia drove for another ten minutes. Coming into town, she passed Merkoff's store. She drove on passed it to the corner parking in front of the café.

Mimi said, "Paxton, let me go check things out. I will tell them I came to see you." Sophia butted in saying she would come, too. "This way we can see who and what we are up against."

After ten minutes, the girls returned. I could see Mimi was pissed about something. Walking back to the car, she told me Yuri told the truth. "There are two police with him, Paxton. Nina is there, also." I thought, why is she there? I smiled at Mimi and said, "You wanted this, so do what you must—I will, too." I looked at Ivan and told him to stay with Sophia.

Sophia said, "Like hell—I am going too; I love this shit."

Mimi laughed, "Wow, Sophia; I have never seen this side of you."

Sophia replied, "Oh yes you have, little girl. Remember when I pushed you against the wall? I was not playing; I would have kicked your ass."

Mimi laughed, "Bullshit, not on your best day."

I said, "Girls, we are here for Merkoff." Walking down the street, Mimi told me Merkoff was sitting at the table. She said the two police were sitting on the other side, facing the door. Nina and some other man were on the sofa. I still wondered why Nina was there.

Sophia said, "Let me go first, just to check it out. Paxton, you wait outside." I had forgotten about Yuri; I told them we should get him out of the car. Mimi told me to leave him where he is. "I told Ivan to check on him and if he wakes up, to knock his ass out again."

Ivan said, "Paxton, how do I do that?" I told him to figure it out. Walking around the corner to my place and passing the store, Sophia started to open the door. From the shadows, a voice asked, "Who are you?" It was another Russian policeman. Mimi closed her eyes and raised her hands—the police went flying into the store wall.

Sophia said, "Damn girl, you are getting stronger." Sophia went through the door and Mimi followed; it was a feeling I will never forget—I had this feeling like electricity flowing through my body. Why this was happening? I could not say. The two police stood as Sophia went through the door; they did not see Mimi. Mimi stepped from behind Sophia; Nina saw her. Nina stood, "You are the bitch I came here for. I am going to kill you for the wrong you have caused me." Nina was cursing Mimi with every breath she took. I tell you, I have never seen fights before like the ones I've seen on Earth. Mimi was laughing at Nina.

Nina said, "You bitch; I will have my revenge—I will show you." Nina ran toward Mimi with a huge knife; sad to say it was a mistake for Nina. First, Mimi toyed with her. The two Russian police laid out on the floor; I was not sure if they were dead or knocked out. Then, Sophia took me by the arm. I turned to see Mimi playing with Nina. She was screaming at Mimi. Nina made a trust with the knife as it flew from her hands. Mimi slapped her so hard that blood flew from her nose and mouth. Nina picked herself up from the floor ran back at Mimi. Mimi slapped her again—this time teeth flew from Nina's mouth and blood was pouring. Sophia and I were so caught up in the fight that we forgot about the two police on the floor. Mimi hit Nina again, sending her to the kitchen floor; she was done for. Sophia and I turned as the two police officers stood, then Mimi hit them with something—I was not sure what it was. This all happened so fast, I could not keep up with it.

Nina laid on the floor, bleeding badly. Hell, I thought it was over. Nina came from the floor with a scream. It was too late for her; Mimi broke her neck. The sound was as if you would break a stick. Mimi never tried to stop. I walked to Merkoff; he was twisting around like he needed to go to the bathroom. He was tied to the chair with a gag in his mouth. I untied him then he stood rubbing his wrists. Looking around, he smiled at me, "Damn Russian police; damn assholes.

Merkoff called the magistrate to come to the store then filled him in on what had happened. Time was slipping away, as we talked for what seemed like hours. Yuri was sent to a facility somewhere. Placing him in a van, he was screaming, "They are aliens." The girls went back to Moscow. At my place, I talked to Merkoff late into the night.

Merkoff said, "Paxton, if I could come with you, what would I do with my store?"

I said, "Merkoff, what would it matter? Give it to Ivan; I assure you he will take care of it. Merkoff, you must let me know; we will leave from Tasha's house at three—Merkoff, this is for real."

Merkoff said, "I have heard you say we will leave the house to another place in minutes."

I said, "No, Merkoff; it will be seconds."

Merkoff said in his heavy Russian accent, "You say Paxton, that we leave, but you have not said where we will go."

I said, "I will take you to my home, Merkoff. Merkoff, my home on Ticoru, it is nothing like here; you will love my world. It is only a suggestion. I will not be here Saturday; if you wish to go, close the store Friday night and come with me to Moscow, where the girls live. Sophia and Mimi will cook a delicious meal. Merkoff, this will give you the chance to talk to Ivan."

Merkoff said, as he started to leave the house, "I will think on this, Paxton." I picked up things from the fight. I walked to the window and look out. I saw Anton looking through the store window. I opened the door and walked outside. I said, "Looking for something, Anton?" He jumped as I approached him. I told him Yuri was not here; he has been taken away. Anton told me that he means to hurt all of us. "How is he planning to do that in a facility?" I asked.

Anton replied, "He will be coming again." I told him to leave; do not come back here. It will not end good for you. Anton gave me a smirk as he walked off. Turning, Anton told me Yuri was in a facility in Istra. I went back to my place, finished up, then went to bed.

One thing here in Vologda was the fact that you could not stay in bed long; the Russian air force would scream by in those jet planes—sometimes it sounded like they were landing on the roof. I was having coffee when there was a knock on the door. I walk over to open the door; it was Sophia and Mimi. They both had a huge smile on their faces. I told them about the meeting with Anton; I told them what Yuri said, that Anton said he was in a facility in Istra.

Mimi said, "I know where it is. I was living in a home not too far from that place when Sophia came for me." Mimi looked at Sophia, "You know it has got to be this way; if we let that bastard live, he will find a way to take everything from Ivan, you know that. Sophia, I will not let that happen. It is the way of the Russian government."

Sophia said, "I know you are right, but I wish there was another way." I told the girls Anton would be back, yet he could cause Ivan trouble. He is in deep with the Russian police. "Do not worry about him, I will kill him myself. I knew from the moment I came here that I had to do that. I will track him down. Yuri will be out tomorrow when they find out he is not crazy. Let him come; I will take him to the house and somehow, I will finish this."

Mimi shouted, "Hell yes, I love this shit!" Sophia only shook her head. The girls left for school as Merkoff was coming to my place. They spoke for a moment, then left.

Merkoff asked about Ivan. I told him he was a family member of the girls. "He would be good for you to leave your store to, if you decide go with me."

From the first time Merkoff and I had coffee, I could tell he was a man that enjoyed his drink. Merkoff sat sipping his coffee, leaving me alone until I was finished with my first cup. No one enjoyed a friendly conversation like me, yet I wanted my coffee if I had it. I first had it on Boldlygo; I loved it. Merkoff finished his first, and I poured another for him. Merkoff smiled, looking up.

Merkoff said, "Paxton, you make good coffee." I thought if Merkoff did not come with us, I truly would miss him. In the time I have been here, I have found a devoted friend;

I think I would miss his Russian accent the most. Hannah knew what she was doing when she sent me here.

When I was on Boldlygo, I remember Leah had a Russian accent. Leah's was not as strong as Merkoff's; Leah had been gone from Earth for a long time. I remember her telling me of the unicorns—of course, I did not believe that until I saw them. I remembered the view from the veranda, looking over the valley that was named thousands of years ago: the valley of the unicorn. Leah laughed out loud, "I told you we had them." I stood with my mouth wide open; I tell you it was breathtaking. I had so many thoughts running through my mind when Merkoff called me.

Merkoff said, "Paxton, you hear me?"

I said, "Sorry Merkoff, I was somewhere else."

Merkoff said, "Yes, I can see this. Paxton, if I come with you, what about the money I have? Do I take it with me?" I told him he would have no use for money.

Merkoff said, "I would have nothing. How would I live? How would I survive?" I told him his rubles, he could not spend; they would be no good on Ticoru. "Merkoff, I will see that you are taken care of; I will make you my personal companion. I can do this, being the son of the king."

Merkoff replied, "Then I must get busy, Paxton. Let us go open the store; I will come with you." I told him that was an excellent choice, "Merkoff, we have got to get busy."

Today, time seemed to drag. I watched the door and every person that entered. I waited for Yuri to enter, and

I knew he would come—the thing I did not know was when. I watched the clock on the wall across the street. The hands on the dial moved very slowly. I did see Russian police twice standing by the building. I also saw a man I have never seem before watching the store. I told Merkoff about him.

"Damn Russian police," he said. "Paxton, he is not only police—he is special police. We must watch everything, Paxton." I was cleaning up boxes when the girls stopped in; I saw them when they came through the door.

I said, "Well, what a surprise! Good afternoon." Sophia had this glow about her. Mimi walked to me, placing her arms around me; I thought, I really like this.

Sophia said, "Time is getting close, Paxton." I knew what she was saying.

Sophia said, "When you come to the house Friday, I have something to tell you."

I said, "Well, Sophia, I can hardly wait." I told the girls about the special police; I told them they must watch what they do. "You are probably being watched. Why they have taken an interest in the store, I could not say. I tell you, Saturday could not come fast enough for me." The girls gave me a big embrace; Sophia kissed me on the cheek. Well, hell—I knew where this was going. I thought, it would be good to be home.

The girls left for the school; it was home for them through the week. Sophia did tell me a new school supervisor would take place Monday. The school was Ivan's—after all, Tasha did start the girl's school.

I continued to clean up. Finally, it was time to close. Merkoff locked the back door and said good night; I said the same as I walked to my place. I was going to take a shower. Passing the window, I saw Anton; he was talking to those policemen Merkoff called special police. I knew now what I had to do—I had to take him out. I placed my shirt back on, watching Anton as he walked down the street. I saw the police walk the other way.

I opened the door not so wide and slipped out. I walked behind the building, standing in the shadows where the light did not show. I walked slowly, so not to make noise. I caught the smell of cigarette smoke. I had smelled it before when Anton would take a break, and I knew it was Anton. I made my way to the street, peeking around the corner, I saw Anton was standing next to a sign. I did not know why anyone would smoke. I can see our talk had no effect on him, now I will do what I must. Whatever I must do, it will need to be done before Saturday.

Walking back to my place, I stopped several times. There were many thoughts running through my mind. Walking inside, I made a sandwich and tea. The longer I sat, the more pissed off I got; I needed to get Anton alone. I could get Mimi to help—then I thought, I would do this myself. I have killed before; killing was a way of survival. Sometimes you must do what you must.

Sleep evaded me; for the reasons and thoughts there were in my mind, I could not sleep. Each time I closed my eyes, Anton was all I could see. I was up and down all night. Finally, it was time to face the day, regardless of how tired I was. Sitting on the side of the bed, I thought I heard a noise. Sitting, waiting—for well...I did not know—then a boom and the Russian air force screamed overhead.

I started to stand when my door blew open and two men rushed me. I met one with a kick to the groin. The other one threw an arm, and I ducked him, knocking him to the floor. Turning around, the one I kicked was trying for the door; I let him go. Whoever this man on the floor was, he was going to regret ever coming here. I walked over to him, and I was pissed off. I will give him one thing: he was brave. He came off the floor swinging. I hit him so hard I thought I had killed him, but I only knocked his ass out. It only took twenty minutes to wake up.

I walked to the stove, made coffee, and was on my second cup when he moaned. I sat the cup down and walked to him. I said, "Asshole, you got one chance to make this right. Tell me who you are and who sent you." He looked at me and spit blood. Blood was also running down his face from his broke nose. In a heavy Russian accent he answered, "You broke my nose." I told him his nose was not the only thing I was going to break unless you answered me. "This I promise you."

He said, "I will tell you nothing, asshole." I slapped him across the face and grabbed him, picking him up and pushing him on to the table on his back. I reached for the coffee pot; I tilted it as to pour it on his face. Damn, I really wanted to do this. He tried to scream, but I had my arm across his throat. He did utter, "Stop, stop." He told me what I needed to know, that it was Yuri.

I whispered in his ear, "You want to live?"

Choking on his blood from his nose, he said, "Yes, please." I told him "You leave here and if I ever see you again, I will kill you." I pushed harder on his throat. "Do you believe me?" He nodded his head as he ran for the door. I watched him as he ran across the lot, and I never saw him again. I walked back to the table and poured another cup of coffee.

These assholes tearing through my door and coming at me before I have my coffee—who the hell do they think they are? I poured another cup and looking around, I saw Merkoff came through the door. He was shaking his head.

Merkoff said, "Damn, Paxton, what the hell happened?" I told him what had happened; I told him it was Yuri that sent them. "Merkoff, I will kill them before I leave. I do not want to do this, but they brought it to me and now I will take it to them."

Merkoff said, "Paxton, you will need help; tell me what I must do and I will do it."

I said, "Merkoff, I want to get them alone. I want them to come to the house, then I will destroy them." Merkoff told me he would do whatever I asked.

"Merkoff, open the store." Today was Wednesday; it was a busy day. Wednesday was always the worst it had been since I had been here. I tell you, Saturday could not come fast enough. All I know for sure is that I do not belong here. I want to go home; it has been so long. Throughout the day, there were so many people coming and going; sometimes I wondered do Earth people work, and if so, where? Merkoff walked to me as we were cleaning up. Merkoff told me it was a particularly good day.

Merkoff prepared to close the store. I told him I was going to my place. He told me as I was leaving that he would see me soon. Merkoff walked in and sat down. I poured him a glass of tea. He smiled at me and with that accent he said, "Paxton, I have noticed you have not drank here." I told him I was not a fan. He insisted on a drink with me, so I agreed on one. Merkoff took a valse from his pocket. He asked for two small glasses. Pouring something in the glass, I asked, "Now tell me friend, what is this?" Smiling, he replied, "Vodka. Let us drink to mother Russia." I must admit it was rough going down; it reminded me of a drink I had on Rigel. I did not want more.

Merkoff had two more, then smiling said: "Paxton, if we are leaving, why do we work so hard? I think you are bullshiting me."

I said, "Merkoff, if that is what you believe, let us leave tonight. We can go to Moscow, and we can stay at the girl's house. I will ask Ivan about taking over the store. It will also give you the opportunity to talk." Merkoff had another drink; I could see he was thinking. He placed his hand to his face. Merkoff said, "What about all my things?" I told him to leave it. "I promise you, Merkoff—you will not need it." Merkoff contacted the girls. I told them what we were doing. Sophia told me to go and they would see me tomorrow night. Gathering a few things from the store, Merkoff and I left for Moscow.

CHAPTER 16

TIME COMES AND GOES. IVAN STOOD OUTSIDE MY room, calling to me. I looked at the clock beside the bed: it was five-thirty. I answered and thought how nice it was not to hear the Russian jets fly over. He talked to me through the door; Ivan told me him and Merkoff were going to the store. After the talk we had last night, he had decided to take a chance. Merkoff told me he was going to give Ivan some pointers.

I told them to have a good day. I turned over and went back to sleep. I was sleeping well, I thought. A quaint noise woke me. I lie still for a moment to listen; I heard nothing else. I was wanting a cup of coffee. I sat on the side of the bed and put my clothes on then heard that noise again. I could not be sure what it was; it was coming from the kitchen. In my thoughts, did the girls come home early? Looking at the clock, it was eight- thirty in the morning; someone was in the house. I stepped softly to the door and eased it open just enough to look out. Creeping around in the kitchen was Anton. I thought, how lucky can I be? Opening the door I saw Anton staring at me, and the look on his face was unbelievable. Looking straight into my eyes, Anton said: "You! What are you doing here?" I told him I live here.

I had picked up a fire poker, the one that you stir a fire with. Anton made a run for the door; I would say he could move but he did not make it to the door. I threw the poker and it hit him through the midsection of his body. Looking up at me, Anton said, "Please, help me." Replying, I said, "Anton, I told you to leave; you refused and now you are in my house. You are dying, Anton—nothing I can do for you." Anton died on the living room floor. I had no feeling about this at all. I did call the Russian police; it was all I could do.

Shortly after I contacted the police, they arrived. I told them of the many incidents Anton and I had. Two hours passed and finally a police officer told me to stay home in case they wanted to talk to me. I told him I was not going anywhere. Yuri showed up an hour later. He told me he had come to detain me—well, I knew better. I told him I wanted no trouble; just leave me alone. "You and the police have harassed me since I arrived here in Russia," I said, "just leave me alone."

Yuri replied, "Or what? Are you threating me?"

I said, "Yuri, you do not want to go there with me. you sent Anton here; he told me before he died that you sent him."

Yuri said, "Who do you think they will believe, you over me?"

I said, "Yuri, I do not need anyone to believe me. Look, if you do not leave me alone, no one will find you." Yuri had an unbelievable look on his face as he came closer, "You do not threaten me; I am Russian police." I told him I did not care who or what he was. I told him he could die as quick as any man.

Yuri stomped the floor, "This is not over with." I told him it better be. Yuri told me he would be back.

Today was Thursday, so two more days and I will be gone. I thought as he left: bring it on, asshole. I thought all day as I cleaned up the blood from the floor, I was thinking how I would love to be home on Ticoru. It has been eight years since I left. Look what I have done, the places I have been. In my thoughts, I wanted to settle down. I wanted Sophia to come home with me; I wanted her to be my wife. I have never told her about my world. Tasha told her about the other life, of what they call their earth family. Before we leave, I will ask her about this, maybe even tonight.

Thursday morning passed into Thursday afternoon. I was sitting in Tasha's big chair; the sun coming through the window felt so soothing. My mind was light-years away when I heard someone come through the front door. The sound brought me to the floor. The girls were home from school. Sophia called to me and I answered back. "I am in Tasha's room." Both girls came to me with a warming embrace.

Sophia asked, "Well, sir, how was your day?" I told the girls I had killed Anton. "I killed him by the front door. I called the police, and they came and removed the body. I was cleaning up when Yuri showed up. I told him if he did not leave us alone, he could die as fast as Anton. Yuri left quickly, telling me he would be back. You know I hope he does, and I hope it is before Saturday."

Mimi said, "I'm telling you now, that asshole has got to die—I mean it."

Sophia asked, "Well, busy man, where is Ivan?" I told her about Merkoff and how he was leaving everything to Ivan. Smiling, Sophia said, "Well, that's the way it should be." Mimi was still beside me, as she knew what I was about to say.

I said, "Sophia, the way it should be is we need to be on Ticoru. We should be looking from our veranda at the ice caps. We should be husband and wife."

Sophia dropped a plate that shattered into a hundred pieces. She placed her hands on her hips.

Sophia said, "Is this a proposal sir? If it is, I accept."

I said, "Well, I did not think it would be that easy! Sophia, it is the answer I was looking for."

Mimi asked, "Ok, now what happens to me?" I told Mimi she had three or four choices: she could stay here, go to Galaxo, go to Boldlygo, or go to Ticoru.

Mimi said, "I want to see them all before I make a decision." I told her that was an excellent choice.

Sophia said, "This is Thursday; Mimi and I will not be returning to the school." I told her they could only take the clothes they were wearing, nothing more. "Everything you have here on Earth, you will have no use for. You must leave everything with Ivan. You will need no money or personal things. Everything you wish for will be there for you. Here on Earth, you see women wearing makeup. If you see this on other worlds, it is to enhance the beauty that is already there. I promise you; if you wish for makeup, it will be there for you.

"Mimi, you are going on seventeen. On other worlds, you will be of childbearing age—this only means you are of legal age. If you come to my world, I will introduce you to a family member."

Mimi asked, "Do they look as good as you?" Well, I did not know what to say. Personally, I thought I was average.

I said, "Well, I do not know how to answer that; I did not know I looked good."

Sophia said, "Yeah, right." "I am serious," I said. "Mimi, you are an exceptionally beautiful young woman. Mimi, I am not sure; however, if DNA were performed, I would say you, Leah, and Adair somehow shared the same DNA."

Sophia said, "What about me, do you think I am beautiful?" I walked to her, took her in my arms, and kissed her for the first time. I felt her go limp in my arms.

I said, "Did that answer your question?" Sophia replied with one word, "Damn." Mimi and I laughed out loud.

Merkoff and Ivan came in at about seven. I filled them in on the events of the day. Merkoff told me Yuri had been standing outside the store all afternoon. "Paxton, I will not be going back; it belongs to Ivan now, he is a fast learner."

Dinner was served and we had a delicious meal; everyone was enjoying the evening in peace. The conversations were good. The time was getting late, so I told them I was going to bed. Merkoff said he was going to bed, also. I started to my room when Sophia took my hand, leading me to her room. I took her in my arms and asked, "Are you sure you want to do this?"

Sophia said, "I have never wanted anything more than this." I looked over my shoulder; Mimi give me two thumbs up. Being with Sophia was all I expected it to be. Sophia fell deeper in love that night, and so did I. On my world, I have been with other women, but not like this. It was a feeling I have never had and will never forget—Sophia would be my love forever. Waking up on Friday morning lying beside her, I thought nothing could be more pleasant than this. Sophia and I showered and went to the kitchen for coffee. Time was counting down; soon it would be time to go.

I sat watching her make breakfast; this woman moving around the kitchen so gracefully was something to see. She was the love I have always wanted; the one I have waited for so long. Mimi broke the silence by saying, "I do not need to ask about your night." I looked at her and she had a smile on her face as big as the galaxy. Sophia told her to hush.

Mimi said in her baby voice, "Oh Sophia, I really want to hear about it."

Sophia said, "Kiss my ass, Mimi," I laid my head on my arms then to the table, snickering out loud. Sophia threw a slice of toast at me. Well hell, that only made Mimi and I laugh harder.

Sophia said, "You two are ridiculous." We started laughing again; I could see us living a long life together. I felt it was going be a wonderful life.

The day moved into Friday night, and there still was no sign of Yuri. Ivan came home from the store and said he did not see Yuri at the store. Sophia was making dinner when Mimi ran into the house. Mimi said, "Paxton, that asshole Yuri is sitting across the street in his car. Let me kill him. I promise you, no one will know it was me. I told her to wait after dinner and see if he is still there. "If he is, we will and must have just a little fun."

Mimi said, "Bullshit; I want to kill him now." Just a quick thought ran through my mind—it was not the first time. I think maybe Mimi and Leah share the same DNA. From what I have seen, they do show similar DNA—doing what Mimi wants to do is also the Leah way.

Sophia and Mimi served dinner. We sat having an enjoyable conversation; I noticed Mimi gazing toward the window. Mimi cleared the table with my help. Walking toward the big window that looked out onto the street, Mimi came back smiling.

Mimi said, "Paxton, that asshole is still there. Can I go kill him now? You know, Paxton, it is like Sophia told you last night—she never wanted anything more."

Sophia said, "Mimi, kiss my ass." Mimi laughed loudly. I told Mimi to go out the back, walk up to him, and ask Yuri what he wants. She did that and more—I watched her as she went to the car. Yuri open the door, then Mimi and Yuri walked toward the house. Coming up the steps into the house, Mimi said, "I told him he could use the bathroom." Well, that was good enough for me and a sign to start. Ten minutes later, Yuri was yelling for someone to let him out.

Mimi said in her baby voice, "Oh Yuri, did the little man get himself locked in the bathroom?"

Yuri screamed, "Let me out of here, you little bitch, I damn well mean it!"

Mimi replied, "I cannot help you ,Yuri; just turn the knob, dumbass." At midnight, Yuri was still pounding on the wall.

Saturday morning, Yuri could hear us outside. Yuri said, "Please let me out."

I walked to the door. I said, "Yuri, if I let you out will you be good? Will you sit and talk to us and tell me why you are doing this?"

Yuri answered, "I will put you in prison for the rest of your life—this I promise you I will." I told Yuri that was not nice. "You started this, I will finish it." Screaming, Yuri said, "You cannot do this, I am Russian police!"

I told Ivan not to go to the store today, I told him he needed to be here when Zin comes. Ivan agreed. Time comes and goes; it was two-thirty in the afternoon—it was almost time to go. I unlocked the door of the bathroom let Yuri out. Opening the door, I took Yuri by the arm and led him to the table.

I said, "Yuri, if you try to cause me trouble, I will have Mimi crush your head." Yuri laughed. I told Mimi to show him. Mimi took a pot off the stove and crushed it as you would paper. Yuri jumped—I swear sweat ran down his face.

Yuri said, "How did you do that? What are you?"

Mimi said, "Yuri, I am an alien. Paxton, what do we do with him?" Suddenly, the wall opened. Yuri saw this and was scared to death. "I knew this all along. I will make life so hard for you." Zin stepped through the portal.

Zin said, "Oh, you have another friend that wants to go." I told Zin as fast as I could. Zin said, "Bring him, I have a special place for him." We said our goodbyes to Ivan, and Zin closed the portal to the house. He opened it on the Moon of Spores where Cavota was waiting. I said, "Zin, the Moon of Spores." The girls were so scared, they had turned the color of the clouds. I held on to Sophia's hand. I told her not to worry; we will leave shortly.

Mimi said, "I'm not scared—I cannot believe this is real." Cavota said, "Don't worry about him; I have a home for him." The portal opened and closed again. Everyone walked on to the courtyard of the palace. The girls and Merkoff fell to their knees, it was such a sight to behold. Tears filled their eyes. Everyone came to meet Mimi, the last living person of the earth family—a journey that started hundreds of years ago, with Maoke and Bota. There would be a feast tonight; Mayrra and Ra would be there.

Zin said, "Come, make yourselves at home. We will talk about your future planes tomorrow."

THE END

This will conclude the book, titled *I Do Not Belong Here*. It also will end the Galaxian series and Boldlygo. I do have another book that I have not published yet of stories in the same universe.

A word from Carl Sheffield, the author: I started my journey in 2017. I love writing. My granddaughters tell me I have a weird, vivid imagination. I absolutely love science fiction—even as a child, the old Flash Gordon and Buck Rogers movies that have been long time forgotten were a favorite of mine. I truly hope you enjoy reading this book, and my other books, also. Maybe I will someday author another book. Maybe even continue this book, *I Do Not Belong Here*, by turning it into a series.

The Staff of Ira series is a four book series.
Childs Book
The Beginning
Mud Bone Baby foot, and Old Ring Paw.
The Journeys of Dorn Part 1
The journey of Dorn Part 2
Salvation.
Ticoru
Galaxian series.
I Do Not Belong Here.
The Search for Icol
Galaxian
The Abduction of Hannah

Milton Keynes UK
Ingram Content Group UK Ltd.
UKHW021104090823
426580UK00015B/432

9 798822 918757